"Now, everyone, lean forward, keep your heads down and keep your hands behind your necks." Dugan fought the plane as it sped toward the island, holding its nose up as the tail dropped.

Bang! The tail slapped the water. The impact sent a tremendous jolt through the plane. The island approached at alarming speed.

Bang! Bang! The plane skipped on the waves.

And then, with a deafening *Boom!* the plane smashed on the ocean's surface. It bounced— almost tumbled—over the water. The whole body of the plane quivered from the shock. Screeches and shrieks and shouts filled the cabin. And Dugan fought for every last instant of control.

There were sounds of tearing metal and breaking wood, frightened animals and terrified people.

And then it stopped. They were unharmed.

WALT DISNEY PRODUCTIONS presents
THE LAST FLIGHT OF NOAH'S ARK

Starring

ELLIOTT GOULD   GENEVIEVE BUJOLD
RICKY SCHRODER   VINCENT GARDENIA

Co-Starring

TAMMY   JOHN   YUKI
LAUREN   FUJIOKA   SHIMODA

Screenplay by STEVEN W. CARABATSOS and
SANDY GLASS & GEORGE ARTHUR BLOOM
Story by ERNEST K. GANN

Co-Produced by JAN WILLIAMS
Produced by RON MILLER
Directed by CHARLES JARROTT

THE LAST FLIGHT OF NOAH'S ARK

A novel by CHAS CARNER

Based on the Walt Disney Productions Film

Screenplay by STEVEN W. CARABATSOS and

SANDY GLASS & GEORGE ARTHUR BLOOM

Story by ERNEST K. GANN

BALLANTINE BOOKS • NEW YORK

All rights reserved under International and Pan-American
Copyright Conventions. Published in the United States by
Ballantine Books, a division of Random House, Inc., New
York, and simultaneously in Canada by Random House of
Canada, Limited, Toronto, Canada.

Library of Congress Catalog Card Number: 80-66169

ISBN 0-345-29173-5

Manufactured in the United States of America

First Edition: July 1980
First Special Printing: July 1980

THE LAST FLIGHT OF NOAH'S ARK

PART ONE

CHAPTER ONE

THE boy sat in the shade beside the old barn and watched a pair of swallows swoop and dart through the hot morning sky. The male bird hung overhead, playing the air with its forked tail; its feathers looked metallic in the sunlight. Suddenly, it dove and banked sharply up and under the eaves of the building and, with a flurry of its wings, hovered a moment before alighting on the edge of a wattled nest amid the rafters. Instantly, the nest came alive with peeps and chirps from three tiny, scrawny babies that opened their beaks greedily and shook their scraggly heads side to side. Patiently, the father bird fed each one and stood over them protectively, awaiting his mate's return with yet more food for the ever-hungry family.

"Come on, Bobby," the girl yelled from across the yard. "Everybody's waiting. All the other animals

are ready and we need you to help with Brutus."
She ran toward the boy who did not look up from
the bristly black-eyed Susan he twirled between his
fingers.

"Leave me alone," he said sulkily.

The girl stopped a few feet from her friend's side.
"Miss Lafleur said they have to leave pretty soon if
they're going to take off today," she said softly,
sensing his sadness. The boy squinted up at her; she
stuffed her hands into her back pockets, smiled and
shrugged her shoulders.

"Sure, Julie, this is real easy for *you*," Bobby
snapped back. "While you were busy trying on a new
set of parents for size, I raised him from when he
was this high." He held his hand at arm's length over
his head. "While *you* paddled around in your fancy
swimming pool all summer, I—" He stopped suddenly and tossed the flower at her feet. Julie knelt
and picked it up.

"Please, Bobby?" she continued calmly. "He's
pretty nervous and he might hurt somebody if they
try to put him on the truck."

Bobby rose and brushed the dust from his jeans
as he walked away. "You mean, he could hurt *himself*," he returned, not looking back. Julie stood
and watched him walk away; he disappeared behind
the tiny chicken coop, heading toward the stockyard. Julie stuck the yellow-and-black flower into a
buttonhole in her shirt.

He heard the ruckus even before he saw them.
"Be careful of his horns, Miss Lafleur," old Miss

4

Braithwaite called from a safe distance, protecting the other children with her outstretched arms.

Miss Lafleur pulled hard on a long rope, the other end of which was attached to the halter of a huge Brahman bull. "Easy, Brutus," Miss Lafleur tried, "no one's going to hurt you. . . ." She dug her heels into the gravel driveway and leaned against one ton of stubbornness. Brutus dropped his head, snorted once and stepped backward. Miss Lafleur dug trenches into the ground with her shoes.

"You'll never do it that way," Bobby shouted. Brutus calmed a bit and looked up at the boy, perking his ears and cocking his head. Bobby approached the towering bull and touched the animal's shoulder lightly. "What are you doing?" Bobby whispered into his ear. "What's Melinda gonna think about all this?" Brutus nuzzled Bobby's chest, almost knocking the boy off balance. "You and your girlfriend are going all the way to Makuarana. Your own tropical paradise!" Brutus licked the boy's hand with his rough tongue. Bobby scratched the bull behind his poll. Brutus tilted his head closer and moved his long horns out of the way.

Bobby turned to Miss Lafleur. "I'll make a deal with you," he began.

"Okay," the pretty woman nodded.

"I'll get him on the truck, but I get to come along to the airport."

"Okay," she agreed soberly.

"And me!" Julie called from amid the other children beside Miss Braithwaite.

"And Julie, too," Bobby added somberly.

5

"And Julie," she agreed with a slight French accent.

"And I get to ride in back."

"Okay. Deal."

Bobby ran his hand along the bull's neck. "Don't be afraid," the boy soothed, "I'm coming with you." Bobby could feel the animal's muscles relax under his loose skin. Brutus took a step toward the wooden ramp. "Come on," Bobby coaxed. And Brutus followed the boy up the steep incline and into the high-sided truck.

Julie walked right behind them. "Good boy, Brutus," she said, patting the bull on his cheek. Brutus ate the flower from her shirtfront.

"What d'you want to come along for?" Bobby asked. Julie stuck her hands into her back pockets, smiled and shrugged.

Miss Lafleur drove southwest, toward San Diego, keeping the big truck on the back roads. It was a long ride, but none of her passengers seemed to mind. Brutus and Melinda lay in the fresh straw, chewing their cuds and nearly dozing. Two fat pigs grunted and rooted in the corner. The sheep and goats appeared a little anxious, as did the ducks and chickens in their cages, but they all remained calm and relatively quiet.

"I wonder where we are?" Julie asked, standing atop a couple of bales of hay and peeling back the canvas cover.

"Beats me," said Bobby, lounging against Brutus as if the bull were a sofa, hands behind his head, feet up, eyes closed. Sunlight flooded the back of the truck and the boy smiled, feeling the warmth on his face. It was easy for him to pretend that he and his friend were back in the hillside pastures above the orphanage.

"Somewhere on the edge of the desert," Julie interrupted Bobby's thought. "It's pretty, come look," she urged. Bobby rose with a sigh and climbed up the side of the rattling truck. He poked his head over the top; the wind blew his blond hair straight back.

The narrow road wandered over gently rolling hills, and the afternoon sun stood high overhead. Up ahead, in the distance, Bobby could see the tall saguaro. The branches of the towering cacti sported beautiful white blossoms. Behind them, through the shimmering heat, the Santa Ana Mountains rose in the north.

"My father came from around these parts," Bobby said, almost to himself. "He used to tell me stories about camping out in the Joshua trees and looking for gold with some old prospector named Denby. . . ." Bobby gazed out toward the east.

"Did he ever find any?" Julie asked as they climbed back down and sat on the bales of hay.

"Uh-huh. Enough to make this ring for my mom." He dug through his jeans pocket and produced a tiny suede pouch. Carefully, he opened it and shook out a tissue-wrapped wedding ring.

Julie took it between two fingers and held it to the light. "It's beautiful!" she exclaimed. Dozens of thin golden threads had been woven together to form a delicate band.

"She left it to me before she died," he said. "My dad made it for her himself." He felt proud.

"That's what I want my father to be: creative and generous," said the girl, placing the ring in the palm of Bobby's hand. He put it back in the pouch and retied the strings, making sure it was safe in his pocket before responding.

"Well, your last foster parents must've been generous. They were rich enough, that's for sure." He sounded a bit sarcastic.

"At least I try," Julie defended herself. "It's not my fault we couldn't get along. At least I tried to be adopted."

"But those people wanted to adopt you." Bobby felt his patience wearing thin. "You were the one who didn't want *them*."

"My new parents have to be just right," she returned wistfully. "We'll have a perfect family and we'll be happy all the time," she declared with a confident nod. Julie paused a moment and smiled to herself. "He'll be so handsome," she continued, "and she'll be beautiful and gentle and patient and funny—sometimes. . . ."

"Don't forget 'creative and generous,'" Bobby cut in. Julie decided not to notice.

"Smart, too. They'll be real smart and they won't have jobs that make them work late or travel a lot. . . ."

Bobby sighed, shook his head and hopped down from the stack of hay bales. It's no use arguing with her, he thought. "Wake me when we get there." Bobby curled up on an old blanket in the corner and pretended to fall asleep. Julie sat and watched the

8

boy for a long moment. A tiny black lamb stood beside her, fluttering its long woolly tail and tugging at the laces of her shoe.

"Is everything still all right back there?" Miss Braithwaite asked. She peered into the back of the truck and squinted through road-dusty spectacles.

"Yes, ma'am," Bobby answered sleepily from his blanket in the corner. He brushed the hair back from his eyes. Brutus and Melinda rose slowly. Julie yawned and stretched and sat up against a burlap sack of grain.

"Well, guys, we're here," Miss Lafleur called as she opened the back doors wide. A caged rooster crowed at the sudden light.

Eagerly, Bobby scrambled from the truck. "What the—?" He looked in all directions. Scrubby vegetation and desert surrounded them. The truck stood at the end of a single, arrow-straight strip of macadam that stretched due west into the mesquite and sand dunes. Off to one side stood an aging, dilapidated hangar. "You call *this* an airport?!" he asked the young woman.

"Now, Bobby," Miss Lafleur tried cheerfully, "a humble charity organization like the Universe Society can hardly afford to fly all these animals, provisions and equipment to a Pacific island *first class*. We're nonprofit, you know."

"So's this place," Bobby returned sarcastically.

"And it looks like this guy could use some charity," Julie added, pointing over her shoulder with her thumb. Looking behind them, they watched a scruffy old man amble toward them from a sheet-metal shack.

"Is this safe, Bernadette?" Miss Braithwaite asked Miss Lafleur. There was concern in her voice.

"Oh, of course," she returned happily. She approached the old man with her hand extended.

He wiped his hand on his grimy overalls before shaking hers. "Miss Lafleur," he said politely with a snaggletoothed grin.

"Mr. Stoney, I'd like you to meet Miss Braithwaite, Miss Julie Brand and Master Robert Slattery. They're from the Wainwright Orphanage."

"So you folks raised all these critters for Miss Lafleur, eh?" he asked easily.

"All the children at the orphanage helped," Julie answered.

"But some of the kids did more work than others," Bobby added, shooting Julie a look.

"Well, I think it's a fine thing you're doing for all those natives out there on that island, giving them all these animals for food and all—"

"What!" Bobby cut in defensively. Miss Lafleur placed a calming hand on the boy's shoulder.

"The Makuarana Islanders are hardly 'primitive natives,' Mr. Stoney," the woman explained. "But theirs is a fishing culture."

"And there aren't enough fish anymore in their part of the ocean," Julie said, continuing the explanation.

"The big factory fishing ships . . ." Miss Braithwaite added.

"If all this were mere food," Miss Lafleur motioned toward the Nativitylike scene inside the truck,

10

"we would feed a hungry people for a day. But if we teach them to *raise* their own food with these animals, then we have fed them forever."

"With these animals, they can start whole new farms of their own," Julie added. Stoney scratched his chin and pondered their words.

"So, Mr. Stoney, shall we get ready to take off?" Miss Lafleur asked after a pause, startling the old man.

"Well . . . er . . . we're . . . ah . . . having a little bit of a problem finding a pilot."

"I beg your pardon?" she gasped.

"Now, don't go getting yourself all upset, Miss Lafleur," Stoney tried. "That's not as bad as it sounds. Why, there're dozens of qualified free-lance pilots in these parts, it's just that I haven't called 'em all yet." The man's attempts to calm her did little.

"We will act according to our contract, Mr. Stoney," she said calmly. "Which calls for us to have these animals and all other cargo loaded and ready for departure by six-thirty this evening."

Stoney looked at his watch. "We will live up to our part of the bargain and shall expect you to live up to yours," the woman continued.

"Let me get back to the office an' make a few more of those calls," Stoney said as he scuffed back to the shed.

"Good," Miss Lafleur smiled, "we wouldn't want to have to ask for our six thousand dollars back."

"Heavens, no!" Stoney chuckled uneasily. He slammed the screen door behind him.

11

Miss Braithwaite looked at her pendant watch and giggled. "T minus eighty-five minutes and counting!"

"I'll wager we'll take off by six-thirty-one!" Miss Lafleur joked.

"At the *latest!*" Julie said triumphantly.

Bobby shook his head and walked away; he kicked a stone that skipped ahead of him. Julie started to call to the boy, but Miss Lafleur stopped her. They watched Bobby as he approached the gigantic, ramshackle hangar. He pushed hard against one of the huge doors until there was just enough space for him to squeeze inside and he stepped into the darkness.

"Let's unload the animals on our own and give Bobby a little time to himself," Miss Lafleur suggested. She lifted a large wooden plank and began to assemble a ramp from the back of the truck.

The tarpaper-and-tin roof of the hangar covered an area of tarmac half the size of a football field. It was cool and quiet and very dark inside the building. Slashes and spears of sunlight pierced through cracks and knotholes and streaked the shadows. And there, in the middle of the echoing space, seeming to fill the hangar wall-to-wall and floor-to-ceiling, stood the largest machine Bobby had ever seen. The boy stared at the gargantuan airplane as if mesmerized. Its wings cut a broad horizontal surface through the sun-speckled darkness ten feet above the ground. Each wing supported two engines, each of which was larger than an automobile. Four engines, four four-bladed propellers. The cigar-shaped body of the plane was almost as long as the wings were wide. Its riveted steel surface was dented and rusty, but Bobby thought the aircraft looked proud and grand. Slowly, he stepped toward the glass-domed nose of the old bomber and peered up and into the cockpit.

"That's a B-29, young man." Stoney's voice came from behind Bobby who turned around quickly. "They called that baby a 'Superfortress.' One of the finest pieces of hardware ever made by man." Stoney came close and patted the plane affectionately on its front landing gear. Bobby looked down along the plane's long underbelly and stared up into the open bomb-bay doors.

"See these engines?" the old man continued. "Each one's over two *thousand* horsepower. She's got a wingspan of one hundred forty-one feet and is ninety-three feet long. She'll carry twenty thousand pounds and fly two thousand miles between fill-ups." Stoney chuckled. "I guess you could say this old girl'll take you and your friends just about anywhere you want to go!"

Miss Lafleur opened one of the big hangar doors and motioned to Julie and Miss Braithwaite to follow her. They came, herding Brutus and Melinda, the sheep and goats and pigs, into the hangar. A pair of white geese waddled along behind and flicked their tails side to side.

"Well, Mr. Stoney," Miss Lafleur said with a smile, "how's our pilot situation?"

"Well, ma'am, I haven't found anyone available yet," he tried.

"Then I suggest you keep trying. Time's a'wasting!"

"Oh, of course." Stoney scurried back to his office. Bobby approached and reached for the bull's halter. "Well, Brutus, my friend," he whispered, "what do *you* think?" Brutus answered with a low moo.

Miss Lafleur scurried to the side of the plane and looked into the opened bomb bay. "We'll need a ramp," she said to herself.

The great airplane had been designed and built to fly at very high altitudes on its many missions during World War II. Because of this, the interior of the bomber had had to be pressurized for those flights into the high, thin air.

"Now, when we flew these planes that high," Stoney continued, "and we opened up the bomb-bay doors to the outside, what do you suppose happened?"

"All the air went out," Bobby answered.

"Exactly," the man replied with a groan. He stopped pushing the heavy crate for a moment. It sat at the top of the ramp, just inside the plane's belly. Bobby and Stoney rested a moment and looked around the cavernous interior. He pointed overhead to what appeared to be a large pipe that ran the length of the fuselage along the ceiling.

"That tube—that backbone sort of thing up there—is a tunnel that connected the pressurized compartments for the crew. We'd crawl through there to get from one to the other."

"Were you a pilot?" Bobby asked the old man.

"Navigator," Stoney said proudly. "It was my

job to take 'em out and get 'em back. . . . The pilot
I talked to a couple of minutes ago—the guy who's
taking this run—he's a veteran, too."

"World War Two?" Bobby asked.

"Nope, he doesn't go back as far as I do, but he
flew in Korea. . . . Another war before your time,"
Stoney added, almost to himself.

"So we do have a pilot, Mr. Stoney?" Miss Lafleur
asked from the base of the ramp. She looked up
from a welter of assorted boxes and a cageful of
chickens.

"Yes, ma'am," Stoney smiled. "He's on his way
here right now."

"Good!" She sounded pleased and shooed a goat
up the ramp ahead of her. "We're right on schedule."
She turned and walked out of sight. Bobby and
Stoney tied the crate securely into place.

Julie picked up armloads of fresh straw and spread
them over the floors of the makeshift stalls.

"I claim the window," she teased the boy.

"Huh?"

"I get to sit next to the window when Miss
Braithwaite drives us home," Julie explained.

"Big deal," Bobby returned flatly.

"You're going to ride in the middle?" Julie asked,
sounding a bit shocked.

"Nope."

"In the back?"

"I'm not *going* back," Bobby whispered.

"What?!" she gasped.

"I'm going with Miss Lafleur." Bobby sounded
very determined.

"Uh-oh . . ." was all Julie could say.

CHAPTER TWO

"THAT'S no plane, Stoney," the angry voice boomed, "that's a pile of *garbage!*" A tall man stood behind them; he stepped closer and jabbed a finger at the old man's face. "If you think I'm riding *that* antique *anywhere,* you're—"

"Dugan! Right on time!" Stoney tried to appear casual. He hurried to the younger man's side and pumped his hand.

Dugan yanked his hand away. "What in God's name—?!"

"Missionary work, Mr. Dugan!" Miss Lafleur shouted from the door. "Missionary work. And we need your help."

Stoney interrupted, "Miss Lafleur, this is Noah Dugan, one of the best pilots I know. He just happened to stop by—I mean—he just happened to be *available* to accept this assignment."

"I see, Mr. Stoney," Miss Lafleur nodded. "Now, Mr. Dugan, what seems to be your complaint?"

"My complaint?!" Dugan shot back. "Lady, that plane would kill me if I tried to fly her! That's my *complaint!*"

"Oh, my!" Miss Braithwaite gasped.

Stoney cleared his throat and hurried after Dugan as he stormed out the door. Julie stepped out of his way just in time. "Well, what do we do now?" she asked.

"We lead the animals aboard the airplane," Miss Lafleur said with conviction. "Our plan is resolute."

"I think he's handsome, don't you?" Julie asked Bobby.

"Stoney?!" Bobby laughed.

"No. The pilot, Mr. Dugan," she answered patiently. "I think he's very nice-looking."

"La-dee-dah!" Bobby mocked. He walked away and helped Miss Lafleur push the two pigs up the ramp and into their stalls. Brutus watched calmly. Julie walked outside and stood near where Dugan and Stoney were arguing.

"No wonder you haven't been able to find a pilot for this job!" Dugan shouted. "There's no one stupid enough to try to *fly* that scrap heap!"

"Now, Dugan," Stoney tried, "we've known each other for too long—"

"Don't try to con me, Stoney," Dugan shot back.

Julie looked past the men and watched a long black limousine pull up and park at the far edge of the airfield. Surprised, Dugan watched two men step out of the shiny automobile and lean against its hood; arms folded, they stared across the field at the pilot.

One of the men was short and nattily dressed; the other tall and threatening-looking. Dugan clenched his fists, swallowed hard and turned back to the old man.

"Dugan, my boy," Stoney continued, placing a fatherly hand on the man's shoulder, "word is out that you've been playing the horses with a singular lack of success." Dugan looked back at the skinny silk-suited little man and his hulking henchman as Stoney continued. "It strikes me that you're in big trouble."

"You son of a sea cook!" Dugan shot back angrily.

"You got no job, no family. None of your buddies has enough to bail you out."

"Stoney, I—"

" 'Cept me." Stoney smiled back at Dugan. Dugan looked back at the men and the limousine. They continued just to stand there in the distance, watching.

"See the slimy little guy?" Dugan asked the old man with a nod toward the silk suit.

"Yep."

"His name is Benchley. See the goon beside him?"

"Yep."

"His name's Coslough. He's Benchley's *pet*."

"Uh-huh," Stoney grunted, poker-faced.

"Last night, on credit," Dugan continued, "I put down five grand on Attaboy Star to win in the ninth. At ten-to-one odds."

"And?" Stoney asked, interested.

"He wins!" Dugan's face brightened. "I go to bed with Benchley owing me fifty thousand dollars!"

"Then how come . . . ?" Stoney pointed toward Benchley and Coslough.

"Seems Benchley doesn't like losing. He got the horse disqualified on appeal. Interference in the stretch."

"Wait a minute," Stoney interrupted. "How'd Benchley——?"

"He does whatever he wants, that's how." Dugan poked his finger into Stoney's belly.

"Oh," Stoney sounded impressed. Julie watched quietly.

"Well, Dugan, here's how I figure it," Stoney said after a long pause. "You either need a lot of money fast or a ride out of town."

"And?" Dugan asked eagerly.

"And I got one of 'em. . . . The quick ride," Stoney added with a toothy grin.

Dugan shook his head. "That's not good enough, Stoney, and you know it. How much am I supposed to get paid for this run?" he demanded.

"That Miss Lafleur, she paid for the whole package in advance. . . . In cash." Stoney looked down at his shoes.

"And I suppose you spent it all already, right? Including the salary for the poor joker who flies that monster."

Stoney nodded sadly. "But I've got something else to offer."

"What?" Dugan asked suspiciously.

"The plane."

"*That* plane?!" Dugan pointed into the hangar. "You think that's *worth* something?!"

"A lot more than you owe Mutt and Jeff over

there." Stoney nodded to the thugs by the car. "In Hawaii, that plane'll sell for ten—maybe eleven thousand. You could drop it off there on your way home. . . . If you *want* to come home."

"What d'you get out of this?" Dugan asked cautiously.

"I've got fond memories of that old girl," Stoney said self-consciously, "and I figure she's got one good mission left in her. You know, one *good* mission?"

Dugan nodded soberly. "I understand."

Stoney continued, "Now, you're the best flyer in these parts, and I figure you're the one who can make sure she makes it all the way."

"Don't try to con me, Stoney—"

"No con, Dugan. I've been calling you all afternoon. How long you been home before I called you?" Stoney pressed.

"This afternoon? Ten—fifteen minutes," Dugan answered.

"I'd been calling you every fifteen minutes all morning, *too!*"

Dugan shook his head and tugged at his ear. "I was out all night celebrating," he confessed. "I thought I'd just won fifty thousand dollars."

"Well," Stoney returned, "this ain't no fifty thousand, but it's a chance to make a clean break—with a head start!" He slapped Dugan's shoulder lightly.

"And I'll send you a muumuu from my new home in Hawaii!" Dugan joked as he shook Stoney's hand. "It's a deal! But we've got to move fast before Benchley finds out."

21

Julie stared at Dugan from the distance, thinking him a very handsome and very brave man.

Julie slipped back into the hangar and joined Bobby and Brutus by the loading ramp.

"Well, where's your 'Mr. Ace Pilot' now?" the boy greeted her.

"Outside with Mr. Stoney," she replied. "They're working out the terms of their agreement." She entered the airplane through the bomb-bay doors and helped Miss Lafleur with the livestock.

Dugan stormed back into the hangar with Stoney hot on his heels. Bobby ran his hand along Brutus' neck and watched the men approach.

"Watch it, kid," Dugan warned, "those things are dangerous."

"Brutus isn't dangerous; he's a friend," Bobby returned defiantly. What was it about the man that he disliked so much? Bobby wondered. The boy stared at Dugan's unshaven face, studied his dark curly hair and avoided looking directly into his eyes. He is not a man to be trusted, Bobby decided. Brutus jerked his head suddenly, startling Dugan who jumped back.

"Watch it, buddy," the pilot warned the bull. Dugan barged up the ramp and into the belly of the plane.

"Don't let him get to you, Bobby," Stoney said. "He's just a lot of talk."

"Stoney, what have you done to her!?" Dugan's voice boomed down from above, startling everyone and every animal. Stoney scurried up the ramp.

"Now, Dugan," he explained hurriedly, "this ship hasn't seen duty for thirty-five years." Julie stopped

22

her work and followed their conversation. "When we converted her to cargo," Stoney continued, "we put in ramp floors over the bomb-bay doors, cut through the bulkheads." Julie followed Stoney's finger as he pointed around the inside of the plane. "To make space, we ripped out the pressurization plant—"

"Hold it!" Dugan interrupted. "No pressurization?!"

"There aren't any mountains over the ocean, remember," Stoney tried with a shrug and a weak grin. "You won't have to take her above ten thousand feet." Dugan gave a sigh of disgust, shook his head and walked toward the cockpit's hatch door.

"Look out!" Julie warned him too late. Dugan clobbered his head against a piece of electronic equipment that dangled from the ceiling by a few wires.

"Are you all right?" Miss Lafleur asked quickly.

Dugan turned and entered the cockpit without answering her. He rubbed the side of his head and Julie and Miss Lafleur followed him in.

Dugan panned over the disheveled cabin. The entire nose of the plane was covered with large windows, some of which wrapped around and even under them. Looking out, Julie felt as if she were standing at the end of a giant tube. She looked through the opened hangar doors and noticed the two men, still standing menacingly beside their limousine at the other side of the field.

Dugan placed his hand on the back of the tattered pilot's seat. "Lady, you're certainly past your prime!" he said.

"I beg your pardon!" Miss Lafleur said; she sounded insulted.

Dugan turned around suddenly; he had not realized that the woman was so near. "The plane. I was talking to the plane," he said. Julie noticed that both Dugan and Miss Lafleur appeared embarrassed.

"What's your name again?" Dugan asked after a long pause.

"Lafleur," the woman responded. "Miss—"

"I mean your *first* name," Dugan pressed.

"Miss Bernadette Lafleur."

Dugan answered her shy smile with a grin. "I'm Noah," he said, "but call me Dugan, I hate my first name."

"I think it's a good name," Julie observed.

Dugan placed his hand on Julie's shoulder and smiled. "Good. From now on we'll call *you* Noah, okay?" he joked. He stepped out of the cockpit and called to Stoney. "Okay, old man, let's get this show on the road! You keep my 'friends' happy outside while Bernie and I get the rest of this stuff ready to roll."

"Bernie?!" Miss Lafleur bridled. Julie smothered a giggle with her hand.

Stoney winked and hurried toward the hangar doors.

"Hey," Dugan called after him. The pilot dug through the pockets of his scuffed leather flight jacket and found his car keys. He tossed them to the old man. "I hear you've always wanted a convertible! Keep her polished," Dugan said.

Stoney smiled. "Thanks!"

"What was that all about?" Bobby asked Julie.

"I'm not sure, but I don't think Mr. Dugan's coming back, either," the girl offered.

They worked quickly. Miss Braithwaite and Julie ushered in the last of the animals and tied them to their stalls. Miss Lafleur placed crates of chickens and ducks in a safe corner. Dugan stacked and lashed down luggage and boxes of provisions.

Bobby and Brutus stood outside the airplane, awaiting their turn to climb aboard; it was Bobby's job to keep the bull calm.

From the first day—over a year before—when Bobby first selected the coffee-gray bull calf in the rancher's stockyard, he had known this day would come. "Everything I care about gets taken away," he said softly to the bull. "Except this time. Nobody's gonna take you away from me now." Brutus nuzzled Bobby's hand.

Dugan stomped down the ramp and placed his hands on his hips, "Okay, kid, let's get that thing aboard," he ordered.

Begrudgingly, Bobby tugged on the bull's halter. Brutus balked. "Come on," Dugan said impatiently, "we don't have all day!" Dugan stepped closer, put both hands at the base of the bull's horns and tugged hard to get the animal moving. "Come on, you ugly slab of meat!" Dugan hollered at the bull. "Get up here or I'll leave you behind!"

"Stop shouting at him," Bobby warned. "Talk slow and easy to him."

"Kid, I don't want to be his friend." Dugan pulled again on the stubborn bull. "I want him in this plane or he'll be riding a barbecue spit before sundown!"

Bobby released his grip on Brutus and let him have his head. Instantly, Brutus dropped his head, snorted once and lunged forward. Dugan, knocked off balance, fell backward against the ramp and found himself pinned to the planks by the angry bull. "What the——!" Dugan tried to squirm free; Bobby caught a glint of fear in the man's eyes.

"Easy, Brutus," Bobby said softly. And Brutus perked his ears and turned back to the boy. Dugan rose slowly. "Keep away from him," Bobby ordered the man.

"Anything you say, kid," he conceded. "Just get the thing on board?" The man tried to appear unshaken.

"Guess we showed him," Bobby whispered into the bull's ear. "Come on, let's go." Dugan stepped out of their way quickly as Bobby and the bull strode casually up the ramp and into the plane.

"Bobby, come say good-bye to Miss Lafleur and Mr. Dugan," Miss Braithwaite called from the bottom of the ramp.

"Yes, ma'am," he answered, giving Brutus a quick hug around the neck. He had hoped that no one would notice that he was still aboard. How would he have time to find another way to stow aboard? he worried.

"Time's running out!" Julie whispered to the boy as they walked under the wings toward the small, opened trapdoor to the cockpit.

Bobby looked up and waved to Miss Lafleur and

Dugan. "Bye, again," he said sadly. Dugan buckled himself into the pilot's seat; Miss Lafleur sat beside him and smiled down at the boy.

"I'll take good care of Brutus for you, Bobby. I promise," the young woman assured him.

"I know," he returned.

Dugan reached to close the trapdoor. "See ya, kids; thanks for your help."

"Bye," Julie said softly. Dugan closed the door.

Miss Braithwaite led the children to the far edge of the hangar and signaled "all clear" before Dugan fired up the first engine. It rumbled, coughed, sputtered and then caught. "What're you going to do now?" Julie shouted over the roar of the engine. Bobby searched frantically for an idea. The second engine roared to life. The air moved around them like a tornado.

The bomb-bay doors! How had he missed them?! In his rush to take off, Dugan had forgotten to secure the doors to the cargo hold. If Bobby were to make it, he would have to act now, he realized. The third engine started. Miss Braithwaite waved at the plane, oblivious to anything else happening around her.

"I'm going!" Bobby shouted.

"But he's already started the engines!"

"Bye!" Bobby called over his shoulder. He darted away, kept low and made his way to the opened doors. He looked back to Julie before jumping up to climb inside. He was surprised to see her running toward him! "Wait for me!" she shouted. Miss Braithwaite, still with her back to the children, waved happily at the people in the cockpit.

The fourth engine washed even more air over

them as Julie and Bobby struggled to climb aboard. Then the plane began to move! Slowly, it rolled out of the hangar and nosed toward the runway. Bobby grabbed at every handhold and tried to pull himself up. Julie ran below, reaching upward toward the boy. Using the support structure as a ladder, Bobby climbed into the plane and secured himself enough to reach for Julie's hand. She continued to run below, just out of reach. The plane taxied faster. "Run!" Bobby encouraged. He could see two men run toward the black limousine at the edge of the airstrip. "Hurry, Julie!" he shouted over the deafening noise. The boy lunged toward the girl and caught hold of her hand.

The engines opened full throttle; Bobby pulled hard and lifted Julie from the ground; the pavement blurred past beneath her. "Hold on!" he shouted. Julie's free hand found a solid hold and she helped to pull herself up. Suddenly, the doors began to move! Dugan had discovered his mistake and corrected it with a flick of a switch. The children scrambled to remain clear of the closing steel plates. The hatch slammed shut. Both Julie and Bobby lay gasping on the floor, exhausted. They could feel the plane lift off the ground and wobble slightly in the air. They lay very still while the plane made a long, low circle over the field.

Through the windows in the tail of the bomber, as Dugan passed directly over the runway, Bobby and Julie could see Miss Braithwaite, Stoney and the two thugs. They were all jumping, shouting and waving their arms in the air, each for his own reason. The kids laughed at the sight.

Suddenly, Bobby realized that the takeoff had frightened most of the animals around them. The place was filled with the noise they were making. Both kids jumped up and put their hands over their ears, "What d'you want to come along for?" Bobby asked. Julie stuck her hands in her pockets and shrugged her shoulders.

They flew due west, straight at the setting sun, so it took a while for night to engulf the plane. And it was a while after that before Julie and Bobby succeeded in calming all the animals.

Julie sat at the tail gunner's window and stared out at the clear night. A full moon hung in the inky blue sky; it looked like a huge silver disk that floated just out of reach. Pinpricks of light appeared from deep space; she recognized the stars of Orion's belt and the North Star that seemed to twinkle brightest. An occasional wisp of cloud reflected a silvery light as the plane glided over it. She looked down through the early darkness and watched the water below. The plane rocked gently side to side, and Julie hummed a lullaby tune that seemed to comfort and calm the livestock. She smiled, pulled the coarse blanket close to her chin and felt happy—in a disquieting sort of way.

Bobby puttered in the corner, working by the glow of a small utility light. Two sections of the now-obsolete crawl tunnel had separated, leaving enough space for a person to squeeze through. He slid a small crate under the opening, stepped up on it and peered into the tunnel toward the cockpit. Brutus watched the boy and calmly chewed a bit of hay.

"What time is it?" Julie asked after a long moment.

"Shhh," Bobby answered. "This is the first time we've been able to hear the engines. Everything seems so *quiet*."

"Just think, Bobby," she began, "we're heading off to a brand-new place—a whole new world, really!"

"I wonder how long we'll be able to stay there once they find out we've come along for the ride?" The boy jabbed his thumb toward the sealed cockpit hatch and the people beyond.

"Once we reach Makuarana, they'll just *have* to let us stay with them," Julie began. Bobby hopped down from the crate with a sigh and rolled his eyes to the ceiling. Here we go again, he thought.

"We'll live in grass huts—no, tree houses! With the ocean all around and beautiful flowers. . . . Paradise!"

" 'And they all lived happily ever after,' " Bobby mocked. "Geez, Julie, will you knock it off? There's nothing . . ." He let his voice sort of fade away.

She'll never understand, Bobby thought. He stared at the pretty girl with sad eyes. He had hurt her and he knew it; he felt ashamed and turned away. She never knew her parents, he reminded himself. She has lived at the orphanage since just after she was born. What does she know about real people in real families?

"Nothing's perfect," Bobby tried to explain. "You've got to fight for what you want. Protect yourself. Because nobody's ever as great as you want 'em to be." There was an edge, a hardness, to Bobby's voice that Julie had never heard before.

"But we can *try*," Julie thought aloud. Bobby pretended not to hear her. He nestled in the straw beside Brutus and closed his eyes.

Julie turned back to the windows, pulled the warm blanket under her chin and watched the moonlight glint off the waves below.

"Good-night, Bobby," Julie said softly.

"G'night," Bobby answered after a long silence.

It had been a long day, Julie thought. And as she drifted toward sleep, she hoped she would not miss anything during the night!

CHAPTER THREE

BOBBY could not sleep, no matter how hard he tried to relax and to clear his mind. Julie's words haunted him, made him uneasy, and he did not know why. "We can try," she had said to him and he felt sad. He had tried to be a good son to his father, he thought. He had been loving and trusting and where had it gotten him? His father had filled him with stories of adventure and travel, of faraway places and unknown people. And, as they drifted from one town to the next, one state to another, Bobby was told that the next stop would be their last; that they were going to strike it rich and settle down and have a home. A real home. But they continued to live in bus stations and train depots and faded little hotels. That Happy Home was always just one stop away.

Perhaps if his mother had lived, he thought. He found her wedding ring and slipped it on his finger, turning it slowly and watching it in the dim light. He had seen a photograph of her once; his father carried it in his wallet. It was cracked and dog-eared and more gray-and-gray than black-and-white, but Bobby knew she had been a very beautiful woman: warm and open and loving, with happy eyes and a generous smile.

When Miss Lafleur first came to the orphanage and sought him out, he remembered he thought she looked very much like the mother he had never known. "Bobby, I understand you are the person I should talk to." She shook his hand and sat beside him under an old oak tree by the barn. He studied her pretty face and felt secure and at home with her. He suspected that even Miss Braithwaite was surprised by the ease of their friendship since she had so often described the boy as a "loner."

Bobby and Miss Lafleur talked most of the morning. She told him of her plan to raise farm animals and to transport them to an island in the Pacific where the people were in danger of running out of food. She told him that her parents had been missionaries in Africa and that she grew up knowing that she would do the same sort of work. Bobby thought her a courageous and generous woman. He wanted to help. He wanted to *try*.

Together, they rode to a nearby cattle ranch and she let Bobby select the bull calf that he wanted to raise. The choice was easy. Brutus selected him by coming up behind the boy and butting him playfully. Bobby still remembered the way Miss Lafleur had laughed at the sight. Standing in the middle of the field, the sun shining on her auburn hair, she looked so very much like the woman in the photograph. The woman who once wore the golden ring he now held in his hand.

He had decided many months ago not to give up Brutus or to say a final farewell to Miss Lafleur. He had known all along that he would stow away on the plane that would carry them to Makuarana and a life together. He did not want to be adopted by strangers; Julie had tried that twice and those attempts had not worked out. Bobby wanted to remain close to Miss Lafleur and the family of animals they had created.

But what he had not counted on was Dugan. Bobby considered him a brutish and mean man: selfish and rude. The boy had seen the way Dugan treated the animals and the way he talked to him and Julie; the man made Bobby angry. And Bobby had not missed the way Dugan glared at Miss Lafleur. While they worked to load up the plane and readied for takeoff, while Dugan shouted orders and strutted around like a big shot, he watched the pretty woman closely. His eyes studied her from head to toe.

No, Bobby told himself again, this man was not to be trusted at all. Bobby would protect Miss Lafleur, Julie and Brutus and the other animals from the man with the cynical eyes: eyes that looked so much like his father's.

The sounds of violins drifted into the cargo compartment through the crawl tunnel from the cockpit. Music! Curious, Bobby rose slowly and brushed bits of straw from his jeans and out of his hair. Julie slept soundly, curled up by the window and snuggled into her woolly blanket. She looked cozy and content.

Carefullly, Bobby tiptoed to the opening in the tunnel, climbed up and slipped inside. Slowly, he crept the length of the passageway; the music and voices grew louder as he neared the front of the plane.

"Do we have to listen to that junk?" Dugan asked.

"Junk, Mr. Dugan?"

"It's boring, Bernie."

"Beethoven was one of the greatest composers who ever lived. Don't you appreciate good music?" she asked patiently.

Bobby edged closer to the opening and peeked inside. From behind them, Bobby saw the pilot sitting in the left-hand seat, holding the control wheel in both hands. Miss Lafleur sat in the copilot's seat. Dugan puffed on a cigar and blew smoke in her direction. Miss Lafleur waved her hand in front of her face to clear the air. In retaliation, she turned up the volume on her small cassette player.

"Okay, lady, I'll make you a deal," Dugan offered. "You turn off that noise and I'll put out this cigar."

"Agreed," Miss Lafleur said with a nod. She snapped off the tape machine. Dugan removed the cigar from his mouth and tapped it out against the floor.

"How's that?" he asked, sticking the butt back between his teeth.

"Fine, thank you," she answered. She stared through the glass-domed nose at the stars and blackness ahead.

"Boy, that was the best conversation we've had

since we took off," Dugan said sarcastically. "Are you always this talkative?"

Miss Lafleur smiled and shook her head. "I'm sorry, but I just can't help but think of the children. It's not as if I'm going away on some vacation, you know; I may never see Bobby or Julie or the other children at the orphanage ever again. I'll miss them. . . ." Her voice just drifted off; she sounded saddened by the thought. Bobby smiled.

"Ah, there are plenty of other kids in the world," Dugan said as a callous attempt at comforting her. Bobby wanted to smack him one.

Miss Lafleur shook her head. "You don't understand," she said. She turned away and looked out the side window.

With a shrug, Dugan pulled a map out of his flight case, opened it and checked a number of coordinates, then looked at his watch and studied a magnetic compass on the control panel in front of Miss Lafleur.

"Well, Mr. Dugan, where are we?" Miss Lafleur asked, not looking away from the window.

"Right on course, Bernie." Dugan smiled. "That Stoncy is the best navigator I've ever known. His flight charts are right on target." Dugan reached toward a panel over his head and flipped a toggle switch. Suddenly, there was a bright flash and a spray of sparks. The plane veered to the right slightly.

"What's wrong?" Miss Lafleur asked, alarmed. "A fire?"

Dugan pulled off his cap and fanned away the smoke and swatted the sparks off his pants legs. He struggled to regain control of the plane as it lurched again to the right. "I don't believe it!" he shouted. "The automatic pilot on this scrap heap just shorted out! It's finished. Kaput!"

Miss Lafleur removed the cassette player from her lap and placed it on the panel in front of her. She took the map from Dugan and studied the complicated lines and vectors. "How can I help?" she asked.

"Well, Bernie, we've got our work cut out for us, but with that compass and Stoney's map there, we should arrive right on schedule, about half an hour after sunup." Dugan stifled a yawn and Bobby realized that he, too, was sleepy. Perhaps he should return to the cargo area and get some rest, he thought.

Turning around in the narrow passageway was a bit of a problem, but as Bobby crawled toward the back of the plane, he could still hear their conversation.

"Don't worry if you get tired, Mr. Dugan," Miss Lafleur offered. "If you'd like to take a nap, I can manage."

"You can fly?!" Dugan asked.

"I've had a few hours of instruction on the mission's Cessna," she explained.

Their words faded away as Bobby climbed down from the crawl tunnel and returned to his bed beside Brutus.

The groaning engines, the squawking chickens, the sounds of frightened animals worked their ways into Julie's dream. Suddenly, she felt herself falling—

very slowly and from very high up. Around her tumbled the animals: Brutus and Melinda, the sheep and goats. She felt strangely peaceful as she watched a rooster keep himself aloft with a frantic beating of his wings. She thought she might try moving her arms, maybe she could glide to earth, she thought. She was not worried; Mr. Dugan will save us, she thought.

"For crying out loud, Julie!" Bobby shouted at her. "Wake up!" She sat bolt upright and found herself sliding on the floor toward the front of the plane. Then, just as suddenly, she fell backward on her elbows as the plane lurched forward and upward. The plane rocked and wobbled in the air.

"What's happening?!" she shouted, looking out the window. It was still dark.

Bobby staggered among the animals, trying to calm them. "I don't know. Is it a storm?" he shouted back. The plane nosed downward again and he was thrown hard against a wooden cage with half a dozen ducks. The cage tipped over on the floor; one mallard escaped and flew about the cargo area, adding to the confusion and frightening the other animals even more. Bobby tried to catch the bird, but it zigzagged through the air, dodging the boy and slipping right through his hands. Brutus and Melinda jerked against the ropes that held them, trying to break free. Julie stopped her attempts at catching the noisy duck and hurried to calm Brutus and his mate. Bobby made one last dive at the mallard before it flew straight into the opening in the overhead crawl tunnel and disappeared.

Catching Brutus by his halter, Bobby held the

bull's head low and prevented the dangerous thrashing of his massive head by holding fast to the bull's nose ring chain. Melinda slipped on the uneven floor and fell to her knees; Julie held her still until the plane regained stable flight.

Trusting Julie to keep the animals under control, Bobby jumped up and squirmed into the crawl tunnel to search for the duck. He was inching along on his hands and knees, following a trail of feathers, when suddenly he heard a commotion in the cockpit.

"What the hell is that *duck* doing in here?!" Dugan shouted. Bobby felt the plane rock slightly side to side. "Get him out of here before I wring his neck!" threatened the angry pilot.

"Leave him alone!" Bobby warned. The boy's voice echoed into the cockpit from the tunnel and startled both Dugan and Miss Lafleur. The boy stuck his head into the cabin. It still smelled of scorched rubber from the malfunctioning autopilot. Miss Lafleur sat rigidly in her seat, looking frightened and embarrassed.

"What the hell's going on here?!" Dugan demanded.

"That's what I was going to ask," Bobby returned, sounding every bit as angry as the pilot. The duck landed on a piece of equipment against the window in the nose of the plane and began pecking at the glass as if trying to escape. Bobby pushed his way past Dugan and picked up the frightened bird; he calmed it by placing his hand over its eyes and stroking its neck. He held the bird under his arm and pressed it against his body, preventing the duck from flapping its wings.

"Bobby, how on earth——?" Miss Lafleur asked.

"How'd you get on board, you little runt?" Dugan snapped. Miss Lafleur reached for Bobby and helped him sit beside her.

"Through the bomb-bay doors," the boy responded.

"You could have been hurt," Miss Lafleur scolded.

"Hurt, nothing, he could've been *killed!*" Dugan yelled.

Julie poked her head into the cockpit from the tunnel. "We knew what we were doing," she cut in. Dugan gaped at the children in disbelief. A smoldering cigar butt dangled from the corner of his mouth. Miss Lafleur wrapped her arm around Julie's waist and pulled her close. Bobby glared at Dugan.

"You almost got us all killed. I thought you were a hotshot pilot," the boy attacked.

"Listen, kid——"

"All Julie and I've been doing since we took off is protect the animals from *you.*"

"This plane's a little old and rusty," Dugan started to explain.

"Yeah, and so are you," Bobby shot back.

Dugan pointed a finger at Bobby's nose. "Watch it, boy, or I'll roll down one of these windows and stuff you through it!" he threatened.

"Mr. Dugan, I hardly think——" But Miss Lafleur was not allowed to finish.

"Listen, Bernie," Dugan snapped, "I've put up with this kid's lip long enough already. I kept my mouth shut earlier because I figured I'd be rid of him as soon as we took off." Dugan turned back to Bobby, his anger growing. "Nobody asked you to come along, boy. I'm stuck with you and you're stuck with me until we get to What-ya-ma-callit Island and I find a way to ship you home. In the meantime, I suggest you remember who's skipper of this ship and learn a little respect while you're at it. Is that clear?"

Bobby stared back at the man coldly, refusing to answer. "I give the orders and you follow them, get it?" Dugan concluded. Bobby stared back pokerfaced.

"Yes, sir, Mr. Dugan, we understand," Julie answered for her friend. Bobby shot her a look of contempt.

"Good," Dugan said with a nod of satisfaction. "Bernie, you and the kids go back and check on the cargo. Make sure the animals are all right and let me get back to driving this bus."

Miss Lafleur unbuckled her seat belt. "Aye-aye, Captain," she said with a mock salute. She rose and took Bobby's and Julie's hands, giving them both a squeeze of affection. Together, they opened the hatch and stepped into the cargo compartment.

"I'm afraid all the commotion a little while ago was my fault," Miss Lafleur confessed. Bobby and Julie looked up at her, confused. The woman sat on a nearby bale of hay and continued. "You see, I had been bragging that I thought that I could fly the plane because I have had a few hours' worth of instruction in a little two-seater airplane that was owned by my parents' mission in Africa."

"But you could have crashed the plane," Julie said.

"I know," admitted the woman, "and I apologize."

"But if Mr. Dugan is supposed to be the captain, then he shouldn't have let you try to fly it," Bobby observed.

"Let's just say that we both learned our lessons and that we're all lucky no one was injured." She placed her hand on Bobby's shoulder. "I made a mistake," she admitted. "I'm sorry."

Bobby turned away and walked among the restless animals, soothing them with a soft word or a gentle hand. He sat cross-legged on the floor and cradled the tiny black lamb in his lap. He watched Miss Lafleur and Julie fashion a bed of straw and blankets. "I'm not sleepy," he told them. "If you can stay up, so can I."

"Suit yourself," Miss Lafleur shrugged. "Why don't you ride up front with Mr. Dugan and me."

Julie yawned and slipped under the covers. She was asleep in no time at all.

Bobby sat at the nose of the plane and watched the horizon turn from deep black to a dark blue.

Miss Lafleur poured three cups of coffee from her large thermos and handed them around. Bobby felt very grown up as he accepted his. Dugan hummed to himself and followed the compass-directed heading due west.

"Listen, you guys," said the pilot, "it'll be sunrise in just about a minute. Come and take a look; it'll be the most beautiful morning you've ever seen." Dugan pointed straight behind them with his thumb. "Just look straight over the tail section . . . keep watching, it happens so fast that you might miss it if you look away."

Bobby and Miss Lafleur followed his instructions. Then the horizon off to their left lightened steadily to a powder gray and then a rosy glow. Suddenly, like an explosion, the sky turned a brilliant orange. Streaks of red and gold fanned out through the sky. Bobby smiled, feeling the new warmth on his face.

"I thought it was supposed to rise behind us." Miss Lafleur's voice sounded concerned. "What's it doing over there?"

"I don't know!" Dugan sounded worried, too. "I can't believe it. It's not supposed to be off the wing, but off the tail. How could I—?"

Suddenly, Bobby realized what was wrong. They were lost!

Dugan checked the compass. "According to this, we're still on course—" The pilot moaned in horror. "Oh, no . . ." Dugan reached over and removed the cassette player from beside the compass. The needle jumped thirty degrees.

"How long has this been here!" he shouted.

"What happened? What is it?" she asked.

"We've been flying the wrong course."

"What do you mean?"

"I *mean* the magnetic tape and the batteries in this cassette player have interfered with the magnetic field of the compass. And that gave us a wrong reading. How long has this thing been lying there?!"

Miss Lafleur shook her head sadly. "I don't know," she whispered. "A long time."

Dugan looked stunned. "We had just enough fuel to get us to your island, and we've burned up most of it flying in the wrong direction!"

Bobby rose and ran toward the hatch. "I'll wake Julie," he said.

"Good, kid," Dugan returned, "and hang on 'cause I'm taking her down to check out the ocean in case I have to make a controlled landing." He pushed the controls forward and the plane made a gentle descent. "Gotta use every trick I know to squeeze out extra mileage," he said to himself. "Please, God, don't make me have to ditch in the sea."

Miss Lafleur prayed softly beside him.

Dugan switched his radio to all channels and spoke calmly and clearly into the mike. "Mayday . . . Mayday. This is flight A-One-Niner . . . Repeat, this is A-One-Niner. Request triangulation . . . Mayday." The radio responded with scrambled static, random pops and hisses.

"What the hell." Dugan slammed down the microphone. "We're so far out of range nobody'll hear us anyway!"

Bobby and Julie joined Miss Lafleur in the corner; kneeling together, hands clasped, they prayed.

"Do you really think that's going to do us any good?!" Dugan shouted over his shoulder at them.

"Do you think it will do us any harm, Mr. Dugan?" Miss Lafleur responded. Her voice sounded peaceful, almost serene.

"Look, soon as you're finished there, get yourselves in the back and make sure every last *chicken* is tied down securely. This ain't gonna be no happy landing!" Dugan's voice meant business. Even Bobby obeyed the order without question. "And then get back up here with me as soon as you can so I know you'll be safe!" he called out after them.

Bobby stuck his head back into the cockpit. "Yes, sir," he said with sincere respect.

Miss Lafleur held the radio microphone in both hands and continued to work the transmitter. "Mayday, Mayday, someone please help us," she called over and over, but with no success.

Bobby knelt in the nose of the plane, panning the horizon with a pair of binoculars. Desperately, he searched for land, a ship, another airplane, *anything*. Nothing but blue water and blue sky could be seen.

Dugan worked the controls and piloted the plane with fingertip precision. His eyes darted from one dial to the next and back to the horizon. He sat ready, poised on the edge of his seat, prepared for any emergency.

Julie dug through Dugan's flight jacket pockets and found a cigar. Like an expert, she unwrapped it, wet it, bit off the tip at the end and lit it with a wooden match. She blew a small smoke ring before sticking it between Dugan's teeth.

"Thanks, bud," he said, not moving his eyes from the controls.

"Don't mention it," Julie said. She picked up another pair of binoculars and joined Bobby at the nose.

For twenty minutes they flew low over the glistening water. The ocean waves were rolling and small; it was a calm sea and Dugan was glad.

Suddenly, the far engine on the right wing sputtered and died. The propeller turned listlessly in the wind.

"We've been running on fumes for about the past three minutes," Dugan said.

The nearer engine on the right choked and coughed.

"Are we going to crash, Mr. Dugan?" Julie asked.

"Don't worry, Julie, we'll make it," he answered. with the cigar held tight in his teeth. ". . . Somehow!" he whispered to Miss Lafleur.

Bobby caught a hint of darkness just below the horizon to the south. He focused on the spot and held his breath. Suddenly, he saw a halo of clouds hanging over the water. "Mr. Dugan," Bobby began cautiously, his hopes building, "turn left."

"What?!" Dugan asked as if the boy were talking nonsense.

Bobby saw a tiny triangle rise at a point on the arched horizon. "Over there, Mr. Dugan." He pointed toward it.

The third engine ran out of fuel.

"Mr. Dugan!" Bobby shouted. "Turn left *now!*"

Still confused, not yet able to see the speck of land, Dugan sensed that Bobby knew what he was talking about.

"Right, kid." Dugan obeyed, following Bobby's finger. Then he saw the small ring of clouds that signaled an island. Immediately, he began to climb the plane. "Kid, you've got the eyes of an eagle. I'm proud of you!" Dugan's words were a true compliment.

"Thanks!" Bobby found himself saying.

Dugan slapped Miss Lafleur on her knee affectionately. "We're gonna do it, Bernie!" Dugan grinned. Miss Lafleur took the cigar from Dugan's teeth and held it nervously between two fingers. She stared at it, then took a puff before giving it back.

"Hurry, kids, strap yourselves into the engineer's seat!" he called. Bobby and Julie scrambled to the seat in the back of the cabin, climbed in and pulled the belt tight. "Good," Dugan said calmly. "Now, everyone, lean forward, keep your heads down and keep your hands behind your necks." They obeyed immediately.

Dugan fought the plane as it sped toward the island, holding its nose up as the tail dropped.

Bang! The tail slapped the water. The impact sent a tremendous jolt through the plane. Dugan pulled hard on the controls and clenched his teeth so hard he bit off his cigar.

The island approached at alarming speed.

Bang! Bang! The plane skipped on the waves.

And then, with a deafening *Boom!* the plane smashed upon the ocean's surface. It bounced—almost tumbled—over the water. The whole body of the plane quivered from the shock. Screeches and shrieks and shouts filled the cabin. And Dugan fought for every last instant of control.

Water poured over the nose as the plane plowed through the waves and skidded toward the beach.

Bobby held onto Julie with all his might and watched as the plane thrust itself upon the beach and pushed its way toward the bordering jungle. He heard the sounds of tearing metal and breaking wood, frightened animals and terrified people.

And then it stopped: the motion, the momentum, the mechanical mayhem.

"Are you okay?" Bobby asked Julie. He looked at a thicket of vines just outside the windows.

"Uh-huh," Julie answered, a bit dazed.

"Bernie?" Dugan asked.

"I'm all right, Noah," she answered wearily.

They were unharmed.

"We were lucky," Dugan sighed.

"Amen," Miss Lafleur agreed.

PART TWO

CHAPTER FOUR

A SUDDEN *Crash!-Crash!* shook the crippled plane from the inside. Brutus' bellowing echoed from the main compartment. Bobby pulled off his seat belt and ran toward the door. There was a sudden *Bang!* of metal against metal. "Brutus!" Bobby shouted, tugging at the latch. "He's hurt!" There came a sound of breaking glass from the other side of the bulkhead.

Dugan clamped a strong hand onto Bobby's shoulder and stopped the boy. "Easy, kid," he warned. Bobby pulled away and began to open the door. "It sounds like a riot in there!" Dugan shouted.

"He's hurt!" Bobby almost cried. "He needs me!"

"That bull's scared out of his wits and he'll pulverize you if you go in there!" Dugan refused to release the boy. Melinda's moo could be heard through a frenzied scramble of baahs and bleats.

Dugan opened a small metal trunk behind his seat and pulled out a long-handled ax.

"No!" Bobby screamed. "Stop!"

Dugan pushed the boy out of his way and approached the hatch.

"I won't use this unless I have to—"

"No!"

Dugan kicked open the door and looked inside. Brutus stood in the middle of the floor, a broken chain dangling from his halter. He faced Dugan, stomped his left front hoof and stared at the man with angry red eyes. Taking a deep breath, Dugan got a grip on the ax just behind its double-edged head and ducked his head to step through the door.

Brutus thrashed his head suddenly, impaling a wooden crate on his horn and ripping it apart. Bobby pushed himself toward the door and called out to the bull.

"Brutus, you have to stop," he pleaded.

Brutus snorted once and dropped his head.

Dugan stood ready for the attack.

"Please, Mr. Dugan, let me talk to him?!" Dugan stood his ground. Bobby moved closer to the bull.

"Everything's okay, Brutus," Bobby soothed. He extended his hand slowly and inched his way forward. Julie and Miss Lafleur crowded at the doorway, holding their breaths, almost afraid to watch.

Brutus cocked his head and flicked his tail nervously. The muscles in the bull's shoulders looked like great ropes under his skin.

"It's over," Bobby continued, softly. "We're safe."

Brutus perked his ears and pawed the floor.

"Mr. Dugan, put down the ax," Bobby said calmly.

"You're outta your mind," Dugan shot back.

Bobby stepped between him and the bull and called out over his shoulder, "I *said* put the ax down!"

Slowly, never taking his eyes off the huge animal, Dugan placed the ax on the floor in front of him. He was very careful to keep it within reach. "Okay, kid," he said after a cautious pause.

Brutus raised his head slowly. Bobby moved toward him and stopped a few feet away. "Come here," he whispered. Brutus stepped to the boy's side. The boy and the bull looked back at Dugan, Julie and Miss Lafleur, who looked stunned and exhausted.

"It's okay," Bobby assured them.

The place was a shambles. Crates of supplies had been torn free of their bindings and been dashed against the floor and walls. Bits of clothing, tools and stores of food were strewn around as in the aftermath of an explosion. The little black lamb lay trembling in a corner. Julie knelt to comfort it.

Chickens and ducks flapped and fluttered and hopped all over the place. Sheep and goats packed together in another space as if hiding. Melinda stared back at Dugan and Miss Lafleur. An eerie silence filled the space; the animals were quiet, almost as if they were in shock, dazed.

Quickly, gently, Bobby ran his hands over the bull's head, neck and ribs; he pressed his ear against his heaving side and listened to the bull's heart and lungs. Carefully, he checked each of the animal's legs and knees. Melinda, too, received a thorough examination. Miraculously, neither animal had been injured. In fact, all of the animals had survived.

" 'Ten—maybe eleven thousand dollars in Hawaii,' " Dugan said to himself through clenched teeth. As he looked at the destruction around him, he felt his anger simmer just under the surface. Julie remembered Stoney's words to Dugan; once again the pilot has gambled and lost, she thought. She looked out the tail gunner's window and saw a narrow strip of beach dividing a calm azure ocean from a steep and gnarled mass of vegetation.

"I think we're in some sort of cove," she told the others. Bobby moved Brutus back into what remained of his stall.

Slowly, Dugan knelt and picked up the ax. Bobby looked up in alarm. "Relax, kid," Dugan cautioned. "I gotta take a look around outside." He stood up and turned to Miss Lafleur. "There aren't any emergencies around here that you can't handle yourself, are there, Bernie?" he asked almost too politely. The woman shook her head.

The man walked over to the bomb-bay doors and began to pry them open with the ax. Bobby found a small crowbar from inside an overturned toolbox and helped. Together, they strained and struggled to force open the doors; Dugan fought to contain his temper as his frustration grew. Finally unable to remain calm, Dugan stomped upon the doors, startling the animals again. Brutus turned quickly. Dugan looked down at the crack between the barely parted doors and then up at the bull, trying to decide on which to use the weapon: on Brutus or the doors. Hatred showed in his eyes.

"You tell your friend," Dugan instructed Bobby, "to keep his cool from now on or I'll lop his horns off and his head along with them." He pried the doors apart all the way and looked down through the opening. Bobby guessed that they were about six feet above the sand.

Dugan dropped through the trapdoor and onto the beach. Bobby waited for the man to stand and then jumped down on him from above. He grabbed Dugan around the neck and knocked him to the ground. Dugan covered his face with his arm and rolled onto his stomach as Bobby pounded and kicked at him. "Stop threatening us!" Bobby shouted. "I should let Brutus smash you!"

"Knock it off, kid, before you get hurt," Dugan warned. Miss Lafleur called to Bobby to stop. Julie jumped onto the sand and pulled on Bobby's arm.

"Stop it!" she cried. "Everybody stop it! Why can't we be *nice* to each other?!" The girl pushed herself away and ran down the beach, sobbing.

Bobby stopped and watched her run along the water's edge. He refused Dugan's offer of a hand to help him up from his knees.

Dugan shrugged and walked away, studying the airplane, taking in the whole scene.

"Bobby?" Miss Lafleur called from above after a long pause. The boy looked up at her, fighting back the urge to cry. "Please help me down?" she asked softly. "You and I have a lot of work to do."

They pulled off their shoes and rolled up their pants legs. With Dugan gone, Miss Lafleur's voice had a soothing effect on the boy. He felt his anger melt away and, for the first time, he noticed the salt air; it felt moist and warm and soft, smelled clean and lush. Bobby closed his eyes, turned his face toward the sun and took a deep breath.

"Feels good to be alive, doesn't it?" Miss Lafleur asked. Bobby smiled and nodded.

Together, they followed Dugan's footsteps around the plane. Miss Lafleur looked around them and shook her head in disbelief. "It's a miracle," she said. Bobby knew she was right.

The plane had slid straight into the middle of a narrow inlet, skidded from the ocean and onto the land with its nose and fuselage digging a deep trench into the sand. Its wings, like huge sickles, had mowed down palm trees, leaving splintered stumps behind and scattering the trunks like twigs.

Damage to the plane was extensive. Both wings had been lopped off in the crash through the trees, and hunks of twisted metal littered the beach all around them. Each wing had been torn in half midway between its two engines. Oil and hydraulic fluid spirted from severed tubes and lines and leaked from smashed crankcases. Steam and smoke hissed from hot, mangled manifolds.

"What a disaster!" Dugan shouted from the other side of the plane. They ran toward the sounds of loud hammering. Dugan pounded on a chunk of metal at his feet. "Worthless!" he shouted. "I can't fly it! I can't *sell* it—!" He slashed at the piece of wing one more time with his ax.

"Really, Mr. Dugan," Miss Lafleur interrupted, "I'm sure we can find a much more constructive use of your energies than throwing temper tantrums."

"All right," Dugan shot back, "what do you suggest?"

"God has given us keen minds and we must use them," she declared. "Positive thinking! We have been spared from death and we will be rescued. I'm certain of it!" The woman picked up a stick and used it like a riding crop. "And, between that time and now, we must seek out food and water, build ourselves suitable shelter, see to the animals. . . ." She pointed to a stand of palms nearby. "We will build a corral right there."

"Aye-aye, Captain," Dugan said with a mock salute.

They took turns keeping Julie in sight. The girl sat alone on a flat rock above the beach, just staring out at the ocean. One more setback for her, Bobby thought, but as long as he could keep an eye on her, he would not worry, he decided.

As the sun rose higher in the sky and the day grew hotter, it became more imperative that they complete the construction of an adequate corral to contain the livestock. Ropes were stretched from one tree to the next to form a large enclosure among the palms. Fronds, branches and pieces of refuse from the plane were used to fashion a makeshift corral. Dugan cut fence posts and rails with his ax and Bobby dug postholes in the hard-packed sand. Miss Lafleur reinforced the stockade with rocks and other heavy objects.

Once the corral was completed, a ramp was constructed from the plane and the smaller animals were unloaded one at a time. They seemed eager to leave the confines of the hot, stuffy cargo compartment and to step into the fresh air. Even the normally uncooperative pigs trotted down the ramp and into the corral without a fuss. Quickly, the old sow found the shadiest corner and lay down with a groan. Her mate nuzzled her contentedly. The sheep and goats circled the area in a herd, as if looking for a way to escape. Gradually, the animals made themselves at home.

Dugan dumped a heavy bale of hay into the enclosure. "Okay, kid," he called to Bobby, "everything's ready. Bring on the beef!"

Bobby climbed into the plane and untied Brutus and Melinda from their stalls. Slowly, he coaxed them down the ramp and into the corral. He stayed with them while they became accustomed to their new surroundings.

"All present and accounted for!" Dugan announced to Miss Lafleur after counting the livestock and securing the gate. He wiped his brow with his cap. "Time for a swim, don't you think?" he asked.

"No," the woman returned flatly, "I think it is time we built adequate housing for ourselves. Nightfall will be coming soon enough." She turned and headed back to the plane, ready to begin the next project with equal enthusiasm. Dugan dropped his hands to his sides and shook his head slowly, watching her.

"Doesn't that woman ever stop?" he asked himself.

The speckled hermit crab darted across the wet sand in sudden, short bursts of movement. It would stand perfectly still for the longest while, poised on the pointed tips of its legs as if waiting for some sort of signal to proceed. It surveyed the area with eyes that moved at the ends of stalks; each seemed to move independently of the other. And, as soon as it decided the coast was clear, it would scurry along as fast as it could until it found another shell.

Having no protective shell of its own, the hermit crab picked among the empty snail shells washed up on the beach. Cautiously, the crab would study each prospective new home, turning it over with its claws, reaching inside. tentatively to make sure it was not already occupied. Sometimes, the little creature would climb inside the shell and sort of try it on for size. After half a dozen fittings, Julie watched the crab adopt a new shell as its own. Secure in its protective, red-striped armor, the now-bold crab walked slowly toward the water and disappeared under the foam.

Everything finds a home of its own, she thought. Why can't I? She felt sad and lonely. Her hopes of a happy life on Makuarana were as shattered as the plane that was once to have carried her there.

She looked over the beach, feeling helpless and heartsick. It seemed desolate and empty. The waves crested and broke close to the shore, lapping it. The beach was horseshoe-shaped and bordered by thick jungle and rocky cliffs. She felt trapped.

As the sun passed over the island and began to drop behind its single peak, she watched long shadows creep out from the jungle and reach toward her. She saw Bobby climb down from the plane and walk slowly toward her. He looked very tired. It took him a few minutes to reach her.

"Feeling any better?" he asked casually, sitting down beside her and flipping a small stone into the water.

"Nope," she answered.

"Well, we sort of made places for us to sleep tonight," Bobby began. "Cleaning up was the worst part."

He had started by sweeping out the cargo area with a palm frond broom, removing the straw and hay and the pieces of smashed crates and boxes. They collected the useless refuse into a pile for a bonfire later that night. Using salvageable boards and other material, they divided the main compartment into three rooms. "It's not too bad," he assured his friend. She appeared not to hear him.

"Listen, Julie," Bobby began. "That guy and I will probably never get along and you'll just have to get used to it. Nobody ever said we all have to be best buddies."

"Where's Mr. Dugan now?" she asked quietly.

"He and Miss Lafleur are off looking for water. We're supposed to stay close to the plane. . . . I hate the way he orders me around. . . ."

Bobby hopped down from the rock. "Come on; let's have a look around for ourselves."

"But Mr. Dugan said—"

"Who cares what he said? He's not my old man; he can't tell me what to do." Bobby sounded determined to do as he pleased.

Suddenly, they heard a crashing noise coming from the direction of the corral. Both turned and looked in time to see Brutus smash his way through the stockade and run off into the jungle. The bull ran in the opposite direction from the one in which Dugan and Miss Lafleur had headed; he ran straight toward Bobby and Julie. Bobby waved his arms and tried to stop him, but Brutus thundered right past the boy, crashed into the underbrush and disappeared into the jungle.

"Brutus! Stop!" Bobby shouted, chasing after him. Julie scrambled to catch up with the boy.

Brutus trampled a wide path through the tangled foliage; the children tripped after him in the underbrush. But the deeper into the jungle they ran, the darker it grew and the ground cover gave way to towering ferns and palms that formed a high canopy over the jungle floor. Bobby could keep Brutus in sight through the trees; he and Julie chased along behind, calling after the bull.

Finally, Brutus slowed to a trot and then moved in a wide arc through the forest. "Brutus!" Bobby called again, out of breath. The bull stopped and turned to the boy. As Bobby reached the animal he grabbed his halter.

"You . . . you . . . jerk!" Bobby panted, exhausted. "What'd you do that for?!"

Julie held the bull from the other side of his halter and spoke into his ear. "You do as you're told or we'll get mad at you!" Bobby and Julie tugged on the halter to lead Brutus home. But then they both stopped, turned and stared at each other. Bobby wanted to go left; Julie wanted to go right. The bare jungle floor was covered with fallen tree trunks and moss. Without the underbrush there was no path to follow, and in the dark shadows, they could find no clue as to which was the right direction.

"Uh-oh," was all Julie could find to say.

They were running out of time. The afternoon grew later and later and the light grew dimmer. They wandered in one direction and then another, never certain which would lead them home.

"Wait. Stop," Bobby said at last. "We're walking around in circles."

"No we're not," Julie said, just as frustrated and tired as Bobby.

"Yes we are; look." He pointed to two sets of footprints in the moss and soft earth near where they stood. Julie examined them closely, then compared her foot with each of the prints.

"Oh, no, we aren't," she concluded. "These aren't our footprints."

"Then whose are they?"

"Beats me," Julie said with a nervous shrug.

"There are people here! If we follow these tracks, maybe we can find out who they are. Maybe we can find out *where* we are!"

"I don't want to, Bobby," Julie said. She sounded frightened.

"Come on, maybe they're friendly and they can help get us off this island."

"Maybe they're not," Julie warned.

"Then Brutus'll take care of us," he said with confidence. "Come on."

Bobby and Julie led the bull cautiously, looking in all directions around them, following the strange footprints.

Suddenly, there was the sound of a tree crashing through the forest. "Look out!" Bobby shouted. It smashed to the ground a short distance in front of them.

They turned to run in the opposite direction when a second tree toppled and cut off their retreat. "Bobby, I—!"

"Stop!" A powerful voice froze Bobby and Julie in fear.

Slowly, they turned around. Julie gasped and Bobby raised his hands slowly.

Before them stood two uniformed men, both armed with rifles. They were older, Oriental men with hard, weathered features.

"No go! No go!" the taller, younger man warned. "This path no for you. No go!"

The older man raised his rifle menacingly.

"Who are you?" Bobby asked in a trembling voice.

"Imperial Japanese Navy," the man announced. "Very strong!"

Bobby and Julie looked at each other from under Brutus' chin. "Uh-oh," Bobby moaned.

"You said it," Julie returned.

CHAPTER FIVE

THE older Japanese sailor spoke no English, but he made his desires well known. Gesturing with his rifle, he directed the children to move away from the bull and to keep their hands over their heads. He spoke to the younger man.

"What did he say?" Bobby asked.

"Commander Hiro say we take enemy prisoner."

"Us?!" Bobby shouted. "What've we done to you?"

Hiro shouted over the boy's protests. Brutus snorted once and dropped his head.

"Better tell him to stop yelling at us. Brutus doesn't like it," Bobby warned, gesturing to the bull.

The younger man spoke to Hiro in his own language. Both men laughed. Hiro stepped closer toward the bull and shouted a challenge at Brutus.

Brutus pawed the ground and thrust his head forward.

The old sailors stopped laughing and began to back away slowly. Bobby swatted the bull on the rump and Brutus lunged at the men. With a scream, they turned tail and ran through the jungle with Brutus in hot pursuit. Weaving through the trees, they scrambled up a small rise and down the other side of the hill. Bobby and Julie followed behind.

They chased the men to the edge of a steep ravine where they skidded to a halt, teetering on the edge. A swift, narrow river poured over rocks twenty feet below them. A rickety rope bridge spanned the chasm right in front of them. Brutus pawed the ground a few feet away and stepped closer. The two men argued briefly, then climbed onto the bridge in escape. Bobby and Julie watched as Brutus hooked his horns into the rope supports and shook it wildly. The two men were tossed side to side, each holding on as best he could. Unable to move from the center of the bridge, the men watched helplessly as the support cables began to pull apart. Thrown suddenly off balance, Hiro fell backward into the river below and pulled his partner in with him.

Bobby and Julie laughed and waved as the two old men were swept downstream, sliding over smooth rocks and dunking into swirling pools farther downriver.

The boy patted the bull proudly. "Let's go see why they didn't want us to go down that path," he suggested, feeling a bit cocky.

The footpath was well worn and the earth beneath their feet hard and smooth; they had no trouble finding their way along it. They soon arrived at a sort of camp.

A thatched-roof hut hid behind a stand of bamboo and a faded and tattered Japanese Imperial flag hung down from a cord stretched between two trees.

"These guys are from World War Two!" Bobby announced.

Cautiously, they circled the hut and studied the campsite. Coals smoldered in an outside fireplace, over which hung a large pot of steaming soup. A vine had been stretched from one side of the hut and wrapped around a nearby tree. Over it were draped frayed, faded shirts and a pair of kneeless pants. A hollowed log held water like a bathtub. And just outside the hut's only door, a ring of decaying sandbags protected a rusted machine gun and belts of ammunition.

A loud whistling sound and a sudden burst of light startled Bobby and Julie. They turned quickly and looked up through the trees. A signal flare arced high through the air and glowed through the treetops.

"That's Mr. Dugan!" Julie shouted, excitedly.

"Come on," Bobby said, tugging on Brutus. "We're not far from the plane!"

With the signal from the beach, the children were able to find their way back to Dugan and Miss Lafleur in only a few minutes.

By the time they reached the beach, Dugan had lit the bonfire and stoked it until the flames reached high into the air. He hollered at them across the sand as they ran to join him. "Where the hell've you been? I thought I told you to stay close to home!" Bobby detected a hint of honest concern in the man's voice even though Dugan tried his best only to sound annoyed.

Miss Lafleur hurried toward the children with arms outstretched. "We've been so worried!" she said as she met them.

Both Bobby and Julie began talking at once, trying to relate the events of the afternoon.

"We were sitting on the rock," Julie began.

"And Brutus escaped," Bobby cut in.

"And we chased him. And got lost. And then the—"

"Hold it! Hold it!" Dugan shouted over their voices. "One at a time, please."

Gradually, the whole story was told. Dugan and Miss Lafleur listened with increased concern.

"Must've been a military outpost during the war," Dugan said. "And they don't know it's over. I've read where the news never reached some of them." Dugan sounded almost as if he pitied the old men.

"Well, then, Mr. Dugan, in that case what do *you* tell them what's what!" Miss Lafleur declared, thinking that a sensible suggestion.

"Are you out of your gourd?" Dugan asked. "They could cut you down before you opened your mouth. Why should they listen to you?"

"Well then, Mr. Dugan, in that case what do *you* suggest?" asked the woman.

"I say we set up shop inside the plane and put a little armor between them and us." Dugan sounded dead serious.

*　　*　　*

Bobby and Julie panned over the beach through the tail gunner's window, searching with their binoculars for any sign of movement.

"Really, Mr. Dugan, I hardly think all this is necessary," Miss Lafleur protested. "Surely these are reasonable men—"

"What's the matter with you, Bernie?" Dugan interrupted. "Didn't you hear what the kids said? Those guys have real guns, with real bullets. And they think *we're* the enemy!" The pilot loaded his wide-barreled flare gun. Bobby hoped the animals would be safe in their corral.

"At least let's *try* to communicate with them," pleaded the woman.

"Bernie, for almost forty years, those men have been waiting for a moment like this. We just crashed on their island in a World War Two, American *bomber*. Do you honestly believe they'd buy your story about making farmers out of fishermen on an island?"

"Look!" Bobby shouted. He pointed toward the edge of the jungle. Julie followed his finger with her binoculars.

"Here they come," she warned. "They've got guns."

The old men approached the plane cautiously, rifles poised and ready, grenades hooked to their belts.

"Surrender!" one man called. "Be prisoner of war or die!"

"You sure you want to go out there and chat with those fellows, Bernie?" Dugan asked. She shook her head.

"Okay, everybody, stay down," Dugan ordered. He followed the movements of the men through the window.

Suddenly, Hiro barked an order to the other man who aimed his rifle and fired.

With a smoky flash, the ancient weapon misfired, exploding the magazine. The gun was thrown to the ground in fright. Dugan and Bobby laughed at the scene.

But Hiro did not think the mishap very funny. He ripped a grenade from his belt, pulled its pin and hurled it. "Cover your heads!" Dugan shouted. The grenade landed directly under the plane, beneath the open bomb-bay doors.

Instantly, Dugan dove through the doors and onto the grenade, scooping it up and throwing it back at the commander and his lieutenant. The men dove for cover.

The old grenade hissed and smoked. It was a harmless dud!

Holding his loaded flare gun close, Dugan zigzagged toward his attackers, taking cover behind one tree and then the next. Hiro took careful aim.

"Get down!" Julie shouted. Dugan ducked as Hiro pulled the trigger. Silence!

Dugan took careful aim and fired his flare. It streaked toward the men with a sulfurous trail and exploded at their feet, blinding them with a vivid red light.

Confused and defenseless, the old warriors retreated back into the jungle. Dugan, looking very proud of himself, blew at the end of his flare gun as a cowboy does his six-gun and sauntered back to the plane. Miss Lafleur applauded his victory.

"Pretty fancy shootin', eh, ma'am?" Dugan kidded in a thick Texas drawl. Bobby thought the man a show-off. Julie thought him heroic.

Bobby and Julie decided to sleep in the "room at the rear"; they liked being able to look out the tail gunner's window. And, as Miss Lafleur helped to get them ready for bed, they watched Dugan patrol the beach around the plane. A series of small bonfires ringed the plane and lit up the area. Dugan paced slowly, back and forth, back and forth, never taking his eyes from the dark jungle. Julie felt secure knowing that Dugan stood guard over them.

"Mr. Dugan was brave tonight," Julie said with a dreamy voice.

"Yes, he was," Miss Lafleur agreed. She smoothed out the blankets on the bed of palm fronds and straw.

"He was okay," Bobby sulked, still watching the man's silhouette by the fire outside the window.

Miss Lafleur sat nearby and tucked her feet under her. She was tired and she rested her head against the wall. "I just wish sometimes," she began, almost to herself, "that people didn't have to be brave by risking their lives against one another. . . ."

Bobby turned and studied the woman's face. She seemed to be looking somewhere far away as she shook her head slowly. Bobby sensed her sadness.

"Well," she said after a long silence, "it's time for me to say good-night. I have to go out and spell

Mr. Dugan on watch." She kissed Julie and gave Bobby a quick hug before leaving.

Bobby watched through the window as her shadow approached Dugan's. They stood close together, then crossed, then stopped. Bobby knew they were facing each other in the firelight; they were talking. Finally, Dugan turned and walked away. The boy heard him climb into the plane from below and settle into his section of the compartment.

Bobby snuggled down under his blanket and, just before he fell asleep, he realized that he felt content, secure.

"Where the *hell* is Bernie?!" Dugan shouted at the top of his voice. Bobby and Julie were jolted awake by the noise and blinked at the brightness. Already it was morning!

Dugan stuck his head into their quarters. "Have you guys seen Bernie? I think she's gone!" Dugan looked as if he, too, had just awakened. He sounded concerned. Bobby and Julie shook their heads. Angrily, Dugan crawled to the trapdoor, searching for his flare gun and finding it.

"I knew it!" he shouted. "That crazy missionary's probably trying to negotiate with those guys! Only now it's for her *release!*"

"Where are you going?!" Bobby shouted after Dugan.

"To find that camp and rescue Bernadette!" he shouted back.

"We can lead you there, wait for us!" Julie called. Both kids hurried to catch up with the pilot.

"This way," shouted Bobby, pointing. Together, they entered the jungle.

Moving at a steady pace, Julie and Bobby led Dugan to the old campsite. They could hear Miss Lafleur's protests through the trees as they neared the hut.

"No, no more, please!" she said.

Dugan crept to just outside the door and motioned to the children to stay out of sight. Suddenly, he stood up, kicked open the door and dove inside with a yell. "Banzai!"

The kids heard a loud crash and rushed to peer into the hut. Dugan lay on his back, having just smashed a low table upon which had been placed an assortment of exotic Japanese delicacies. The Oriental gentlemen had been treating Miss Lafleur to a banquet!

"Noah, look what you've done!" Miss Lafleur scolded. Bobby and Julie laughed as Dugan picked himself up, picking bits of food from his clothing, his hair.

"Him friend, too?" asked the tall lieutenant.

"You mean they weren't torturing you?" Dugan asked, confused and humiliated.

"I'm perfectly fine, Mr. Dugan, can't you see that?" asked the woman. "The war is *over*, remember? . . . Now, Noah, children, I would like you to meet Commander Hiro, of the Imperial Japanese Navy." Hiro stood and bowed. "And Lieutenant Kurishima, also known as Cleveland!" The taller, younger man bowed also. Bobby and Julie bowed in return. Even a dazed Dugan managed to crease at the waist.

"Cleveland?" Dugan asked.

"My mother visit America in 1924. Her favorite city Cleveland," he said with a smile. "Also teach me English."

Dugan tugged on his ear and looked to Bobby and Julie in the doorway. Carefully, with his finger-tips, he selected a beautifully prepared shrimp from his shirt pocket. "Breakfast!" he announced to the room and popped it into his mouth with a smile. The children laughed in response.

In 1942, with his beloved emperor involved in a terrible war in the Pacific against the United States, Cleveland had been assigned to the island observation post along with seven other men. Cleveland had been twenty-one years old. Hiro, the ranking officer, had been thirty.

But that was thirty-eight years ago and they had lived on the island ever since; forgotten, unable to escape.

The lieutenant rose from his seat and poured more herb tea for Dugan, Miss Lafleur and the children. Hiro offered them more fruit and shelled nuts.

Bobby listened closely to Cleveland's story and studied the inside of the hut that had been the men's home for so many years. The floor was clean, bare wood, polished to a smooth satin finish. The walls were constructed of whatever material was handy at the time: wood, corrugated iron, bamboo. It was a cozy home, Bobby decided. Seashells, filled with coconut oil and floating braided wicks, cast a gentle, aromatic light around the room. A single orchid blossom floated in a shallow wooden bowl.

Aircraft spotter charts hung on one wall. A dozen silhouettes of Japanese and "enemy" planes showed views of their different angles: underside, head-on and side profile. Each plane was identified in Japanese. Bobby nudged Julie and pointed to a chart of a bomber.

"That's us," he said, "a B-29." Julie nodded and turned back to Cleveland.

Cleveland and Hiro were the only survivors of the original eight sailors who came ashore thirty-eight years ago. In 1943, a single American fighter plane buzzed their camp and riddled it with machine gun fire, destroying their radio transmitter and killing two men. They moved the camp deeper into the jungle so as not to be spotted from the air.

Later that year, unable to make contact with the outside world and running very low on supplies, two other men fashioned a sturdy raft and attempted to reach the strong westerly currents a few miles off the beach. The raft was torn apart by the rugged coral reefs that encircled the island and kept them prisoner.

Years passed. The squadrons of Superfortresses and P-51 Mustangs disappeared. Sightings of the huge American aircraft carriers and destroyers and troop carriers became increasingly infrequent. It had been Cleveland who dared to suggest that maybe the war had ended. That was eleven years ago.

Eventually, they moved their camp to the other side of the island, at the edge of the beach. A signal fire burned every night, but they were never spotted. "By anyone," Cleveland said with a shrug, "friend or foe."

But within a matter of months after they had established their new camp, a great typhoon swept in with a pounding sea, devastating the island. A tidal wave smashed upon the land and carried off with it their two remaining comrades and most of their possessions.

Cleveland and Hiro had lived in the tiny hut on the hill ever since.

"Surely you tried to escape," Miss Lafleur pressed. "After all those years. . . ."

Cleveland nodded. "Many times," he admitted. But the flimsy wooden rafts and boats they constructed were no match for the vicious coral reefs. Nor were they able to protect themselves from the equally vicious sharks that continually patrolled just off the coast. "We need a stronger vessel," Cleveland said sadly.

CHAPTER SIX

THEY walked back toward the beach, discussing their plight. "I think it's a safe bet we can't just sit here and wait for someone to stop by," Dugan said. "Those poor guys have been here for thirty-eight years and we're their first visitors!"

Miss Lafleur bowed her head and shuffled along beside him. "Certainly there is something we can do." Her voice was almost a question.

Bobby and Julie walked a few feet behind with Cleveland and Hiro, talking with sign language and broken English. The older man fashioned a model airplane out of strips of bamboo. As he walked along, he fitted the wings into place and the tail and then held it up for the children to see. He gave it to Bobby and the boy ran ahead, pretending to fly it ahead of him.

As they reached the beach and the big old bomber was clearly seen, Hiro stopped his approach and called Bobby back. "What is it?" Bobby asked, handing the little plane back to the old man. Immediately, Hiro snapped the model's wings in half, just like the B-29's. He spoke quickly to Cleveland in Japanese and turned the toy upside down. Cleveland bowed and hurried ahead to catch up with Dugan and Miss Lafleur.

"Captain Dugan!" he called. Dugan stopped and faced the sailor.

"Commander Hiro, he say we build boat out of plane." Cleveland sounded excited. Dugan looked confused, but Hiro hurried up to them with the model to demonstrate.

If the plane were flipped over onto its back, the big tail could become a sturdy rudder and the jutting remains of the wings would make stabilizing pontoons, Cleveland explained. Hiro nodded and pointed to his bamboo toy. Dugan took the model and studied it.

"What do you think, Bernie?" he asked.

"I don't think we have much of a choice. I'm sure search parties are out looking for our plane, but we're hundreds of miles off course, maybe even a thousand miles from Makuarana. They'll give up searching before they find us. Chalk us up as 'missing at sea.' "

"That's the way I figure it, too," Dugan nodded.

"We have to help ourselves," Miss Lafleur decided.

Dugan bowed to Hiro and then to Cleveland. "Let's give it a try!" he said.

For two days and three nights they worked around the clock.

A huge scaffolding of bamboo was constructed over and around the plane and heavy ropes of braided vines formed a large sling into which the fuselage was hoisted.

"Tail too long for rudder," Cleveland pointed out. "Water close to shore shallow." Dugan understood what needed to be done. He climbed atop the great plane and stood at the tail section, resting his ax on his shoulder. Taking a wide stance and a deep breath, he swung hard at the tail and sunk the ax blade into the sheet metal. It sliced into the tail with a loud *thunk!*

"I wouldn't want that job!" Bobby observed from below. Indeed, it took Dugan most of the day to cut the tail in half.

In the meantime, Miss Lafleur, Cleveland and Hiro busied themselves with readying the plane for the sea. Using the strength of Brutus and Melinda harnessed together, they pulled the remaining engines from their housings and let them fall onto the beach. The empty housings were sealed airtight with tar, forming large floats on either side of the fuselage. Pontoons.

Bobby and Julie worked inside the plane, cleaning out the hull and sealing up all cracks and seams with pitch and tar.

Using an intricate series of levers and pulleys and all the strength they could muster, they succeeded in

raising the gutted plane upon its sling. The inter-
locking A-frames and supports groaned and bowed
under the weight. Slowly, patiently, they removed
the landing gear's wheels and fashioned them into
a huge cartlike affair, strong enough to support the
plane and to roll it back into the ocean from the
beach. So the wheels wouldn't sink into the sand,
they laid down a "track," made from an assortment
of boards, leading down to the water's edge.

But before the rolling platform could be used, the
plane had to be turned over onto its back! After
many discussions, Dugan touched the side of his
head with his finger. "Yankee ingenuity!" he announced proudly.

Under his direction, they attached a series of
bundled vines and ropes to the end of one wing.
The long cords were run up and over the plane and
over the far edge of the opposite wing. With the
plane cradled just above the ground in its sling, it
rocked side to side with very little effort. Dugan's
standing on one wing and bouncing up and down
made the thing roll to one side. Again, harnessing
Brutus and Melinda, and with everyone pulling together, the great plane tilted up and balanced on the
end of its stubby right wing. Restraining ropes lashed
to nearby palm trees prevented the plane from crashing down onto the beach and smashing its launching
cart beneath it. Slowly, gently, the plane was lowered
into place. The cart creaked and the landing gear
tires pressed their special wooden-plank track into
the sand.

Reusing the many A-frame support structures,
Dugan and Hiro erected a tall double mast and a

wide deck around the open bomb-bay doors that now led into the "ship's" hold. The platform was made of bamboo poles, lashed together to form a wide, sturdy floor above deck.

Cleveland prepared food over the nearby fire and served it up to his friends in coconut shell bowls. Bobby and Julie stored cans of fresh water and fruit on board and helped Miss Lafleur sew together every extra scrap of material and clothing they could collect into the large mainsail they needed for their ship. The pieces of cloth came from blankets and canvas tarpaulins, camouflage nets, T-shirts, signal flags. All were stitched together in a sort of crazy-quilt pattern. Finally, Hiro approached with his beloved Imperial flag in his arms. He held it out to Miss Lafleur proudly.

"Oh, Commander," she said, truly touched by his contribution to their cause.

"Our flag strong," Cleveland explained. "It make good sail. You use."

Miss Lafleur bowed graciously and accepted the offering with reverence.

"I'll put it at the very top of the sail. The place of honor," she promised.

Cleveland and Hiro bowed and smiled.

By the third evening, Bobby could feel every muscle in his body. There was not a single one that did not ache and throb. He sat by the bonfire on the beach and closed his eyes, exhausted. Miss Lafleur came up from behind and massaged his shoulders; her fingers and thumbs worked the knots out of his neck and arms. He let himself relax and sort of swayed side to side. He looked over at Dugan dozing nearby. The man lay in the sand, leaning against the trunk of a palm tree. His hands were in his lap, carefully turned palms up, for they were covered with painful rope burns, blisters and gashes. Suddenly, Bobby's cramped back muscles did not seem so bad.

The boy turned and gazed up at the ingenious craft behind him. In spite of its ramshackle appearance, its funny shape and makeshift mast and deck, Bobby knew it to be a strong and seaworthy ship. He felt proud of the work he had done. He felt important. A real member of the crew!

"We sail tomorrow morning at high tide," Miss Lafleur whispered. Bobby nodded. He was ready for this next leg of their adventure.

The flames of the bonfire flickered and reached up into the darkness throwing sparks, like fireflies, into the air. Julie stood behind Miss Lafleur and gently touched the woman's hair. In spite of what lay ahead for them, Julie felt calm and confident. They had all worked well together and she knew it. She, too, felt proud of their accomplishment. They had worked together as a team, she thought. They had helped each other and encouraged each other and offered suggestions and accepted corrections. And nobody got angry! she thought with a smile. Miss Lafleur reached for Julie's hand and gave it a squeeze.

Dugan stirred awake and opened his eyes after a long and loud yawn. He looked through the flickering firelight and focused upon Miss Lafleur, Bobby and Julie sitting close together. They appeared so peaceful. Dugan smiled at the sight.

From behind him, Cleveland and Hiro approached from the dark beach carrying glowing lanterns and the last of their supplies from the old camp. Dugan rose and joined them. The three men sorted through an assortment of fishing lines and small tools.

"Uh-oh," Dugan said slowly, "what's this?" He picked up an old pistol with two fingers and pulled it from the box.

"Commander Hiro say captain of ship—Captain Dugan—must be properly armed to protect his crew," Cleveland said with a bow. Dugan eyed the gun cautiously and set it back down.

"We'll keep it around just in case, but I remember the last time you guys used weapons. Those guns couldn't protect anything."

Bobby watched the men closely. A few days ago, they were trying to kill each other, he thought. But now, now there are no more enemies. Cleveland and Hiro trust Dugan to protect them, he observed. We all rely upon each other, because no one can make it off this island alone. We need one another, he realized. The thought made the boy feel almost tearful.

The night was peaceful and clear. Bobby and Julie lay upon the former ceiling of the tail section of the former plane. They still looked out the rear windows at the moonlit water.

Cleveland and Hiro squatted beside the fire, making last-minute preparations for the morning's launch. The children could hear their conversation although they could not understand the words. Hiro laughed softly in response to something Cleveland said. Bobby thought it was wonderful that the two men had remained such good friends after all the years they had been stranded together. There seemed to be an unspoken understanding between them that he had never experienced before. Oftentimes, while they had been working on the ship, Bobby noticed that one man would automatically help the other without the other's asking. They shared a closeness normally reserved for brothers, Bobby thought. They trusted and respected each other. They relied on each other. . . .

Julie watched Dugan and Miss Lafleur stroll along the shining water's edge. Both appeared shy and self-conscious as they walked along the silver-lit beach. Dugan stopped and pointed way out to sea, toward the crescent moon. The woman stopped and followed his finger with her gaze and absentmindedly placed a tender hand on the man's shoulder. Julie wished she could hear what they were saying.

"Miss Lafleur likes Mr. Dugan," Julie said softly.

Bobby shrugged and watched the two walk along the beach. "I know," he said at last.

"He's a bachelor, you know," the girl continued. "I heard him say he'd never get married because there wasn't a woman alive that could put up with him."

"Good," Bobby said.

"But I think he's sort of nice."

"Nice?!"

"He's not perfect or anything, but he's smart—and he's brave."

"And he hates Brutus and I'll bet he'd leave him

86

and us behind if he had half a chance." Bobby tried to make his voice sound hard and cynical.

"He doesn't hate Brutus, he's afraid of him, that's all," Julie explained.

"Afraid? I thought you just said he was so brave!"

"Well, he doesn't understand Brutus like you do," the girl continued. "Everybody's afraid of things they don't understand, sometimes."

Bobby rolled over onto his side and closed his jacket close under his chin. He fought hard not to agree with Julie's words. He peeked out the window and watched Dugan and Miss Lafleur closely. Miss Lafleur started to walk away, but the man reached for her hand and turned her back toward him. He stepped closer and kissed her lightly on the cheek. Bobby felt a jab of jealousy.

Pouting, Bobby pulled his collar up around his ears and curled up in the corner. Still the boy did not feel safe with Dugan.

"G'night," Bobby said to Julie. But she did not respond. Already, she was asleep.

The sun broke over the water with a burst of light and warmth. It was a perfect, clear morning: warm, balmy. A steady breeze blew from the west.

Eagerly, Julie awoke and shook Bobby from his sleep. "Hurry," she said happily, "it'll be high tide soon." And with that, she scurried out of the sleeping area, climbed up and out of the bomb-bay doors and onto the wooden deck. Miss Lafleur greeted her, holding a sack filled with coconuts.

Bobby stood in the bottom of the hold and peered up at the woman.

"Good morning, sailor!" she said to the boy. She sounded excited, happy. Bobby helped her stow the supplies in the forward section of the hold and as soon as he had finished, he hurried to the corral with Julie. Together, they began to lead the sheep and goats through the gate, up the ramp and into the plane. Dugan burst out of the underbrush with an armload of palm fronds.

"What are you doing?" he shouted at the children.

"Getting the animals on board," Bobby answered.

"The animals are staying here," Dugan announced.

"What?!" Julie and Bobby gasped.

"It's going to be dangerous enough without them. We've got to save ourselves."

"You mean you're just going to go off and leave them?!" Bobby said in shock and disbelief.

"They're only animals," Dugan shrugged, "they'll be all right." Dugan studied the horrified faces of the children and tried another approach. "Look, I know you like them, but—"

"I *love* them!" Julie stamped her foot in protest.

"They trust us to take care of them!" Bobby shouted back.

"Hey, look, I understand," Dugan said softly, "but we—"

"You don't understand!" Bobby said angrily. "You don't know anything about loving them because you don't even like them! Julie thought you were really nice underneath. She said you were just afraid of Brutus because you don't understand him, but you hate him!"

"Now, wait a minute, kid," Dugan tried.

"You're stuck with all of us and all you want to do

is get rid of us! Julie thinks you're smart and brave, but I think you're mean and selfish!" Bobby stormed away and approached Brutus in the middle of the corral.

Julie looked up at Dugan with tears in her eyes and shook her head slowly. She, too, started to walk away.

"Julie?" Dugan called softly, stopping her.

Dugan held out the stack of palm fronds. "Let's make 'em a real nice bed in the hold, okay?" He smiled shyly at the girl, embarrassed at his selfishness. Julie ran to him and embraced him tightly.

"Bobby!" she called out happily. "We're all going on the boat! Everybody!"

"Brutus, too?" the boy asked in disbelief.

"Yes, kid," Dugan chuckled. "Brutus, too."

As Dugan and Bobby worked to load the animals on board, Cleveland and Hiro made ready the sail and tightened support ropes and adjusted the rudder. Julie and Miss Lafleur found a small can of red paint among the stores of supplies and, very carefully, they painted two words on the bow of their comical ship: "Noah's Ark."

"What's this?" Dugan asked them.

"You like it?" asked Miss Lafleur.

Dugan smiled and mussed Julie's hair. "I used to hate the name Noah, but it doesn't look half-bad there!" he said. He sounded a little proud. "Yeah," he answered with a nod, "I like it! Thanks."

Miss Lafleur smiled and watched Dugan climb the ramp and enter the hold with Bobby.

They made sure to keep the livestock and the supplies toward the front of the hold.

"Cleveland warned me about the currents and coral reefs around this island," he said to the boy. "With high tide and all this stuff up front, we should be able to keep the rudder from catching on the reef."

Bobby nodded. He understood. "And once we're out to sea, we can move the animals toward the back so the rudder can really bite into the water," the boy added. Dugan looked impressed.

"Aye-aye, Captain," he said to Bobby with a salute.

Brutus stomped his front hoof, impatient to get going. Dugan started at the sound and still kept a safe distance from the bull. "Tell your buddy we'll be under way in about half an hour," he joked with Bobby.

The boy sensed something new between them, although he was not yet sure what it was. They spoke more easily. Like Cleveland and Hiro, they did not always have to tell each other everything anymore. Maybe they would cease their arguing, he thought.

High tide hit the beach just before noon and the waves lapped against the tail rudder and washed toward the launching platform beneath the plane. Everything was ready, everyone was set to sail. Except Hiro and Cleveland. They had disappeared!

"Where are they?" Dugan asked, worried. "We have to leave *now*." He panned over the beach and looked toward the jungle. "Are the animals secure?" the man asked Bobby.

"They're okay," the boy answered him.

"Well," Dugan said, throwing up his hands, "they'll just have to swim out to meet us."

On cue, Miss Lafleur unfurled the motley sail. It fluttered in the wind and billowed full. In the bright sunlight, it was beautiful to see.

The wind pushed hard against the sail and started the launching platform rolling toward the water. The ropes holding it in place stretched and groaned. With a quick swing of his ax, Dugan severed the restraining ropes and the great ship began to back into the water, powered by the trade winds.

"Here they come!" Julie shouted and pointed toward the edge of the jungle. She hopped up and down on the deck and waved happily at the two men who scurried across the beach. "Hurry!" she called.

The plane began to float in the water and Cleveland and Hiro waded out to join it. Once fully afloat, the ship moved easily in the water. Hiro and Cleveland stood chest-deep in the waves and pushed hard on the nose, trying to turn the bow out to sea. Dugan jumped into the warm ocean and helped them.

Bobby cast them a line and helped the men climb aboard. Miss Lafleur and Julie stood on the wings and pushed against the bottom with long bamboo poles.

Dugan and the two men stood dripping on the deck, under the full-blown sail with the Imperial flag at the very top. Gradually, the ebbing tide and the steady trade wind carried them toward the open water.

"What took you guys so long?" Dugan asked the men.

"We take care of business," Cleveland explained. "Follow orders."

Hiro pointed toward the rise on the island.

Suddenly, there was a tremendous flash of fire and smoke, then they heard the thunderous roar. A series of explosions burst all over the island, one after another, raining debris into the water and showering them with bits of wood from the jungle vegetation.

"What the—!" Dugan shouted in alarm.

"Orders say, leave island, destroy everything," Cleveland explained with an honorable bow to Hiro. Both men smiled and looked very pleased with themselves.

Dugan turned to Miss Lafleur and the children. "Well," he said ominously, "this is it. We either sink or swim!"

As they cut a path through the waves, heading due east, they watched the island jungle burn behind them.

"Nothing like burning one's bridges!" Dugan observed.

PART THREE

CHAPTER SEVEN

JULIE and Bobby knelt in the cockpit, staring eagerly through the windows in the bow. The nose of the plane sliced its way through the waves much as a submarine might while cruising along the surface of the water. Through the top half of the glass dome, the warm sun shone in on them from the clear, ice-blue sky. A single seagull rode a thermal high overhead and spiraled lazily upward.

But the bottom half of the dome revealed a world neither Julie nor Bobby had ever seen. From just below the glaring and sparkling surface to the light-shimmered sand beneath them, the children watched a shower of silvery minnows dart from their approach. Thousands of the tiny slender fish moved at once, almost as if the school swam in waves itself. Suddenly, the school parted and the fish disappeared to either side. Like a curtain opening, Julie thought.

"Look!" Bobby pointed down and to the right. Giant, jagged horns of coral reached toward them from the bottom. A turquoise-and-pink parrot fish nibbled a piece of the spiny-hard coral with its beak-like mouth. It floated, seemingly weightless, merely fanning the water with its delicate fins. A spiny, spotted-brown lobster crawled back into its den and pulled back its long antennae. The growths of coral reached closer to the nose of the plane, threatening to smash the glass and to tear holes into the hull.

Bobby jumped up and ran into the main compartment through the opened hatch. Julie stayed at the nose and kept watch. "Hurry!" she shouted to the boy. "Move Brutus back!"

Bobby tugged on the bull's halter and led him toward the tail of the craft.

The coral grew higher. "And Melinda!" she called. Bobby had to push hard on her hind flanks to get Melinda to move back to Brutus' side. Bobby herded the sheep and goats into the back of the hold, also.

"We're okay!" Julie called from the cockpit happily. She watched a school of coral-colored, big-eyed squirrel fish swim close and look inside. She laughed and waved good-bye as they floated over the reef.

Bang! The impact of the tail rudder against the barrier reef sounded like the scraping of steel on concrete. The ship jerked to a stop in the water.

From the hold, Bobby could hear Cleveland and Hiro, at the stern, arguing in Japanese. Dugan's thundering footsteps approached over Bobby's head from the bow. And even Julie, from inside the cockpit, could hear Dugan's angry voice. "No, Bernie,

just do it the same way I told you to the *last* time!"
The man sounded frustrated and a little edgy.

The pilot dropped through the trapdoor from
above and acted quickly to help Bobby.

Bobby could tell tempers were fraying in the hot
sun.

"Just get the big one up there first, again, okay,
kid?" Dugan asked.

Bobby obliged easily.

Together, they returned the animals to the front
section of the hold and moved to go up on deck.

"You know?" Dugan wisecracked to Bobby as
they climbed outside, "I did learn that bull of yours
is good for one thing."

"What's that?" Bobby asked cautiously.

"Ballast," the man said flatly. Bobby was not sure
whether Dugan was joking or being sarcastic.

For the third time that day, Dugan, Miss Lafleur,
Julie and Bobby stood out on the wings, inching the
ship over the coral with long bamboo poles. Cleveland and Hiro tried to free the rudder, arguing all
the while. This time, it seemed that Hiro wanted to
try to force the rudder free by working it hard side
to side. Cleveland insisted that the mechanism would
not stand the strain. Bobby listened closely, although
he could not understand their words. Julie eyed
Dugan and Miss Lafleur.

Eventually, a solution was found and agreed upon
and, after two attempts, the men succeeded! There
was a screech and a shudder from the hull, but the
ship moved suddenly forward on its own wind power
and continued out to sea. Immediately, forgetting

that they were not back on the island alone, the two old men cheered and embraced and laughed. Their celebration and their victory made everyone else laugh, too. The sailors stopped their happy chatter and became slightly embarrassed, realizing that others were watching. They bowed quickly, comically, and then they laughed again.

The last obstacle that could have stopped them had been surmounted! Julie skipped back into the hold and hurried back into the cockpit, eager to see more.

Bobby climbed midway up the mast and looked back at the island. It seemed so far away from where he stood above the water. The pointed rise appeared so small; a column of black smoke still rose from the jungle and faded away into the sky. Bobby looked down at the others on deck. Dugan and Miss Lafleur stood shoulder-to-shoulder toward the bow, looking out toward the horizon ahead. They held hands.

Cleveland and Hiro stood shoulder-to-shoulder at the stern, looking back at the tiny island that had been their home for so long. Together, they bowed silently, turned their backs on their past life and grasped the rudder control together and set the ship's course.

From back inside the cockpit, kneeling in the domed nose, Julie motioned for Bobby to rejoin her. She pointed down below the water's surface.

An angry moray eel slithered partially out of its rocky lair and snapped its powerful jaws; it was careful to keep a safe distance beneath the gigantic form floating overhead.

Slowly, the clear blue water beneath them grew

deeper and deeper blue. The ocean floor sloped away to blackness. And a giant, batlike eagle ray flapped its powerful wings and escorted the "Ark" into the open sea. Then calmly, as if in slow motion, the graceful ray banked right and dove deep, out of sight.

By sundown, the prevailing winds had stopped. Miss Lafleur's pretty quilt-sail hung limp and lifeless from its mast. Bobby and Hiro climbed the rungs and made the big square sail ready for the night; carefully, they rolled it from the bottom up and tied it to the supporting horizontal boom. Bobby held tight to the mast and watched the old sailor fill his lungs with rich salt air with a contented smile. It was quiet and calm, the ocean smooth. The boat barely rocked with the gentle waves. Hiro climbed higher, to the crow's nest, and pointed into the setting sun. The western horizon glowed a golden-red. They watched the top crescent of the sun drop behind the arc of the vast ocean. And, just as the last piece of the sun disappeared into the distance, just for a fraction of a second, Hiro and Bobby watched the sky flash a sudden iridescent green. Bobby looked surprised, but Hiro smiled and nodded knowingly.

The sky turned deep blue with the coming night.

Bobby and Hiro helped each other climb down from their perch above the others on the deck. Dugan and Miss Lafleur tended a flickering hibachi fire toward the bow. They talked quietly; he snapped twigs in half and dropped them into the glowing fire pot. She stirred a small can of water, waiting for it to boil. Julie sat close by them, using Dugan's pocket-knife to peel and chop bamboo shoots.

Cleveland stood beside the pontoon on one wing. He ran a fishing line through his fingers and dipped it into the water. Slowly, he bobbed it up and down.

Bobby approached the man and selected a fishing line of his own. He baited the hook with a tiny piece of raw fish.

"What was that?" Bobby asked Cleveland, motioning to where the sun had just set behind them.

"Green flash?" Cleveland asked. Bobby nodded. "Sometimes, when sun go down over ocean, and weather just right, green flash happens," Cleveland explained slowly. "Light play trick on eyes. A good sign," he assured the boy, "a happy sign." Bobby smiled and dropped his hook into the water.

Hiro tied off the rudder at the stern and tugged on a few rope lines to test their strength. He seemed to approve of their condition. He panned the horizon for a ship or plane. The water and sky around them were empty.

Bobby felt a nibble on his line. He pulled up quickly. "Missed it!" he hissed.

"There plenty more fish left in sea," Cleveland kidded. Bobby chuckled at the old remark.

After a day filled with hurrying and hard work, arguments and anxieties, Bobby was grateful for a moment of solitary quiet.

"My dad and I used to fish at night," Bobby began, more to himself than to Cleveland. "There was a lake up in the hills near a ranch where he worked one summer. . . . I was only a kid. Three or four."

He paused and stared down into the water. "We used to hang a lantern over the water and the fish would come toward the light."

Cleveland patted Bobby on the shoulder. "My father was fisherman, too," he offered, not fully understanding Bobby's story. "We caught squid at night with lights. Good idea!" The man handed Bobby his line and crossed to where Hiro stood nearby. They talked quietly for a moment and the older man bowed once and climbed down into the hold. He returned with two coconut-oil lamps and lit them; he placed them at the edge of the wing.

Bobby, Cleveland and Hiro sat over the water and dangled their fishing lines into the lighted water.

They caught three small fish.

With great ceremony, Commander Hiro cleaned them and wrapped each one in leaves. He roasted them over the glowing coals in the hibachi.

Later, when the dark night air grew cooler and calmer, they sat in a circle on the foredeck and ate their meal out of coconut shell bowls with rice and stir-fried vegetables. Cleveland taught Bobby and Julie how to use chopsticks.

"I could never use those things," Miss Lafleur confessed. Dugan began to show her how to hold the chopsticks in one hand and to work them with her fingers.

She began to protest, but Dugan cut her off. "You're so good at being the teacher," he observed patiently, "now watch and listen like a good student." The woman nodded.

Julie watched them for a moment and looked toward Bobby. He shot her a glance and looked a bit sleepy and sad.

Morning comes quickly out on the ocean, Bobby realized. With no mountains or hills or trees to block the horizon view, when the sun comes up, it really comes up! he thought. He tended to Brutus and Melinda and the other animals, giving them hay and water and slipping a few pieces of fruit into the bull's rationed breakfast.

Julie fed the chickens and ducks and carefully selected five light-brown eggs from their nests in the straw.

With fresh water so precious, the animals were allotted only a small portion of the water they would ordinarily drink during the day. Bobby knew that Melinda's milk production would decrease to next to nothing over the next few days, but this morning the cow needed milking. Bobby knelt beside her and placed a pan under her swollen udder.

"Isn't this crazy?" the boy called to Julie. "Here we are in the middle of the ocean, in an upside-down airplane, and I'm milking a cow and you're collecting eggs!" Gently, he squeezed and worked his hands on the cow's teats; the milk sprayed into the pan in fine, pulsing streams. "It sure beats living at the orphanage!" he added with a smile.

"And how!" Julie agreed. "An adventure!"

Cradling a wooden bowl filled with the eggs, she climbed the bamboo ladder out of the hold and onto the deck.

Even though the sun stood low in the sky, the air was hot and stagnant. Julie squinted up at Dugan and Hiro on the mast, adjusting the sail, trying to find even a hint of breeze that would carry them to their destination or rescue. They found none; the sail sagged uselessly.

Cleveland and Miss Lafleur knelt close together at the stern. Before them, a faded and crumbling navigational map had been unrolled: one of Hiro's from the war.

Julie approached them and listened.

"Last night," Cleveland began, running his hand over the map, smoothing it out, "Commander Hiro, he studied stars and found our location." The woman studied the large map of their portion of the Pacific. The Hawaiian Islands were right in the middle of the map. She saw where currents flowed and islands jutted out of the sea.

"Where are we?" she asked, hopefully.

"Here," Cleveland answered. He stuck his finger at the lower right-hand corner of the map. Julie saw nothing but plenty of blue paper around his finger.

"That means we're hundreds of miles away from Hawaii!" Miss Lafleur groaned. For the first time, Julie sensed despair in the woman's voice.

Cleveland nodded sadly. "Yes."

The boat drifted aimlessly over the water, rolling in the gentle waves, Helplessly, they waited to be caught by the wind, a current, *anything* to get them moving! And still the boat just sat and bobbed in the water.

Julie was grateful for the late-afternoon clouds that slid by overhead; they temporarily blocked out the glaring sun and cooled the air.

"Some adventure!" Bobby said sarcastically. He watched Hiro and Cleveland trying their luck with the fishing lines. Neither man had caught a fish all day.

Dugan sat on one wing and dangled his feet into the water; he dipped down with his cap, filled it and poured the cool water over his head. He felt helpless and frustrated.

With a sigh, Bobby entered the hold and found Miss Lafleur seated in a corner, reading her Bible and listening to soft classical music on her small cassette player. "You're sad," Bobby said, breaking the silence.

The woman nodded. "I was thinking a while ago that I'm the one who got us all into this mess in the first place."

Bobby stared back at her questioningly.

"I'm the one who came up with the idea of bringing farm animals to the Makuarana Islanders," she continued, feeling sorry for herself. "I'm the one who got you and the other children at the orphanage to raise all these poor creatures."

"But we *wanted* to help," Bobby comforted. She smiled and placed her hand on the boy's.

"I know, and I thank you. . . . But nobody helped me to force Mr. Stoney to pack us all in this ancient airplane and for poor Mr. Dugan to have to fly us off to Never-Never Land." She switched off her tape machine and held it up. "And this—*my* tape recorder—jinxed the compass. . . ." She closed her Bible and held it in both hands. "I keep hoping for a miracle of some sort to get us out of this mess. . . ." The woman shook her head and sounded very tired.

"We're still together," Bobby offered. "That's sort of a miracle, isn't it?"

The pretty woman studied the boy's face and bit her lower lip before smiling and embracing him. "Yes!" she returned, relieved. "I'd say that certainly *is* a miracle!"

"Stop!" Julie shouted in fear. "Don't!"

Bobby helped Miss Lafleur rise and they scrambled up on the deck to see what was wrong.

"Just lure the fish closer, Julie, so I can harpoon it!" Dugan called.

"No!" Julie screamed.

Dugan stood out on one wing holding a slender, sharpened bamboo pole as if it were a spear. Julie knelt at his feet and tugged at his pants leg. "Stop!" Bobby and Miss Lafleur hurried across the deck.

Just off the side of the boat, just out of reach, a sleek, slender porpoise "talked" to them in a language of happy clicks and whistles. Its ever-present smile beamed up at Dugan trustingly.

"Let go, Julie," Dugan warned.

"No!" Julie, Miss Lafleur and Bobby all shouted at once. They startled Dugan so much, he almost fell into the water. The porpoise chirped and splashed at the water.

"What the—?" Dugan sounded annoyed.

"You will not harm that animal," Miss Lafleur ordered. Bobby could tell she was getting her old spirit back.

"That fish?!" Dugan asked, confused. He pointed at the dolphin. It flicked its snout into the water and splashed Dugan's feet.

"That no fish." Cleveland stepped into the scene.

"He's right," Bobby said. "He's an animal, just like Brutus, just like . . . like *you!*" As if in response, the porpoise stood upright in the water, backpedaled quickly and flopped into the waves.

Dugan looked angry and embarrassed and frustrated. He slammed his spear down and barged past Miss Lafleur and Bobby. "I don't know what it is with you people!" he bellowed. "We've got a barnyard full of food right below us and we can't *touch* them! We ate the last of the fruit and today's eggs and what was left of the milk! Nobody's been able to catch a single fish all day and now you tell me I can't kill a dolphin so we can have *supper!*" He slammed his way down into the hold. The sound of his clanging the cockpit hatch echoed on deck.

Julie leaned over the edge of the wing and touched the gentle porpoise with her fingertips. "I'll be right back," she told her new friend. She stepped past Bobby and Miss Lafleur and followed Dugan's route into the hold.

"Mr. Dugan?" Julie tapped on the metal door into the cockpit.

"What?"

Julie stuck her head inside. She saw Dugan sitting on the floor, leaning against the left-hand wall and staring outside through the domed windows. She entered and sat down beside him. The happy dolphin floated just outside, peering into the cockpit from under the water and rolling over slowly. Julie smiled and waved to the inquisitive animal.

"Do you ever get scared?" she asked the pilot after a pause.

"When I'm flying?" Dugan asked.

"No," Julie said simply. "I mean, when you're all by yourself or when you're somewhere you've never been before or when you don't understand something? Do you ever feel scared?"

"Why're you asking me that?" Dugan stalled.

" 'Cause I think you're the bravest man I ever knew," she replied honestly. The porpoise tapped at the glass beside her. She put up a hand to stop it.

"I suppose so," Dugan admitted after a long silence. "I guess everybody does."

"Well," Julie started slowly. "I guess I'm scared now." Dugan wrapped a strong arm around her shoulders and pulled her a little closer.

"Promise you won't tell anybody?" he asked.

"Yep," Julie answered.

"Not even Bobby?"

"Promise."

"I think I'm a little scared myself," Dugan confessed softly. "I'm not used to worrying about a lot of other people. I've always only had to look out for myself."

Julie knew that Dugan did not expect her really to understand, but she did. "We'll take care of each other," she promised. "You'll see!"

Dugan smiled at the girl and kissed the top of her head. He turned and tapped at the glass where the porpoise still waited just below the surface. "If one can love a bull, the other can love a porpoise!" Dugan chuckled.

Suddenly, the happy dolphin righted itself in the water from its lazy rolling. It tensed and turned, then sped away with a flick of its tail.

"You scared him!" Julie pouted.

Bobby's voice echoed around them. "Shark! Shark!"

"Gotta get topside!" Dugan said quickly. He dashed out the hatch, leaving Julie behind.

The girl turned back to the domed windows just as a huge tiger shark opened its mouth inches away from the glass! Julie screamed and jumped back. The shark peered into the cockpit as it swam by.

Julie raced out of the cockpit and onto the deck. "Shark! Shark!" she yelled.

The shark slowly circled the ship. Through the clear water, they watched its huge, shadowy form slither slowly around them.

"It's a tiger shark," Dugan said. "Probably sixteen—eighteen feet long. . . ."

They all stared out at the water. As the sun sank in the west, casting a blood-red light upon the water, the shark's dorsal fin sliced through the glistening surface. Slowly, deliberately, the killer fish moved around them. Silently. Patiently.

"Let's hope nobody rolls out of bed tonight," Dugan said soberly. " 'Cause *he*'ll be close by to wake us up!"

CHAPTER EIGHT

At first light, they all gathered on deck to check the water. Still there was no wind. Still they drifted helplessly on the ocean. And still the menacing shark's fin knifed through the water around them.

"We won't catch any fish today, either, if we don't get rid of that shark," Dugan said.

"Is true," Cleveland nodded. "Either he eat or scare all fish away." Hiro picked up Dugan's spear and jabbed it at the water.

"It's him or us!" Dugan declared.

Bobby found a strong length of rope and handed it to Dugan. Dugan took the harpoon from Hiro and attached the rope to it with two tight knots.

"Okay," Dugan said seriously, "this could get messy, so I want everybody else to get below."

The shark swam closer to the boat, its tail thrashing faster through the water. Dugan followed it with his eyes. "If everything works out all right, we'll have food for a week!"

Bobby helped Miss Lafleur and the others to enter the hold. He watched Dugan standing alone atop one pontoon: harpoon poised, ready to strike.

Julie ran into the cockpit to watch from below. Suddenly, the ferocious tiger shark darted past the windows. Its mouth was opened wide; it streaked toward the surface.

Bang! Dugan's bamboo spear plunged deep into the shark's back, just behind the dorsal fin. Seemingly unharmed, the great fish jerked to one side, and swam away. It dragged the harpoon, the uncurling rope and a trail of blood behind it. Instinct made the shark flee.

It quickly ran out its length of rope and the cable pulled taut with a *twang*. Julie and Miss Lafleur watched the shark turn in the water, readying itself for an attack against its assailant.

Bobby stood just at the top of the ladder, refusing to climb into the hold. He would not let Dugan face the shark alone, he decided. Dugan held tight to the rope and tried to tie it to the pontoon; it tugged and jerked in his hands.

Suddenly, Dugan slipped on the wet metal surface of the wing and almost fell into the water! Bobby ran across the deck to help him.

But the bamboo deck was slippery. The boy could not stop in time; he skidded on his heels and fell into the water!

Below deck, Julie saw the shark react to the sudden splash. It turned quickly to the right and began to make a long sweep of the area, searching for its prey. To one side, she saw Bobby, kicking and clawing his way toward the surface amid a cloud of bubbles.

"Bobby!" Dugan shouted. He released the rope and dove into the water to protect the boy. Yelling loudly, Dugan splashed at the water and flailed his arms, hoping to frighten away the wounded shark.

Miss Lafleur gasped and pushed her way out of the cockpit and past Cleveland and Hiro in the hold. Frantically, she yanked open the metal footlocker beside the base of the ladder and rummaged through it until she found the flare gun. Quickly, she loaded and cocked the weapon and, pointing it upward with one hand, she climbed out onto the deck.

Outside in the water, Dugan swam quickly toward the boy. Whenever he took a breath and looked ahead of himself above the surface, he could see the shark, cutting a straight path toward Bobby who struggled to keep his face above water.

Finally, Dugan reached the boy and grabbed him under his arms. He tried to push him up, toward the surface. As the man looked up, he saw the shark's head rise out of the water; its flat, lifeless eyes glared at him, its mouth opened automatically, exposing hundreds of jagged sawteeth. Dugan pulled the boy close to his chest and waited for the man-eater to strike, hoping he would be hit first.

Suddenly, like a streak from below, the porpoise rocketed upward and rammed its hard snout into the shark's tender belly. The shark, injured and defenseless, retreated into the depths.

Hiro and Cleveland scrambled onto the deck and tossed out lifelines to Dugan and the boy. The man made sure Bobby had a firm grip on one of the ropes before signaling the two men topside to pull him in. The dolphin swam right behind Bobby, pushing him along with his head, guiding him toward his friends who stood ready to pull him aboard.

Dugan, weighted down by sodden clothing and shoes, strained to swim back to the boat. Desperately, he grabbed for a lifeline, but he was always just inches out of reach. Julie and Miss Lafleur called to him to swim harder. "Don't look back!" Julie shouted.

The shark had returned for a counterattack and it swam straight toward Dugan! Once again the porpoise butted the deadly fish, but this time the shark kept right on coming. Miss Lafleur raised the flare gun with both hands and took careful aim. Dugan called for help. The shark was within a few feet of striking.

Bam! Miss Lafleur pulled the trigger. The burning sulfurous ball streaked toward the water just over Dugan's head and exploded into the shark's gills.

There was a sudden spray of sparks, a loud flash of water, smoke and steam, and the murderous shark stopped dead in its own wake.

Dugan hardly had time to realize what had happened when Julie, Hiro and Cleveland burst into cheers and rushed to embrace the trembling Miss Lafleur.

"You did it!" Julie shouted. "You saved him!"

Bobby lay on the wing, exhausted and out of breath, but he reached out as far as he could to grasp Dugan's hand. Behind the gasping man, the dying shark turned slowly in the water and sank beneath the blood-clouded waves.

Bobby and Miss Lafleur pulled Dugan from the water and back onto the wing. He flopped himself onto the deck, gasped for air and coughed out the words, "You . . . you . . . you . . scared me to death!" he panted at Bobby.

"I'm sorry!" Bobby almost begged for forgiveness. "I was trying to help." They reached for each other; Dugan held Bobby by his shoulders and pulled him close in a tight embrace. "I thought I'd lost you there for a minute," he whispered into the boy's ear.

"So did I!" Bobby returned.

Equally exhausted, Julie leaned against Miss Lafleur's side as the woman placed a comforting hand on the girl's shoulder.

"Nice shootin', Bernie," Dugan said with a weak-but-sincere smile. She winked back at him, held up the flare gun and blew at the barrel as a cowboy would with his Colt .45.

"Shucks," she said with a grin. " 'Tweren't nothing."

Dugan scooped up Bobby into his arms and carried the boy below deck; Dugan's legs felt weak at the knees and Bobby's body trembled from fear and exhaustion.

"Take it easy, kid," the man soothed. Bobby wrapped a weak arm around Dugan's neck and held on.

Miss Lafleur and Julie followed them into the hold and helped to tuck Bobby into a warm bed where he shivered under his covers and struggled through a frightening dream: he found himself beneath the cold water's surface. Waves broke around him and covered his face; he fought to keep his head above water. But slowly, steadily, he sank. He felt weightless and helpless. No one could help him and only the brightly colored fish floated all around him, calmly, curiously, watching the boy as he dropped toward the bottom. He tried to kick his legs, to move his arms, to swim upward, but he could not move at all!

"Dugan!" the boy called out in his sleep.

Julie, Miss Lafleur and the pilot sat nearby. The man leaned forward and placed a gentle hand on the boy's brow. With his fingertips, he brushed the hair away from Bobby's face. "I'm right here, kid," he whispered. "Everything's all right." And Bobby stopped his struggling. The boy opened his eyes and focused on Dugan's face and into the man's eyes: the eyes that once had frightened the boy. But now, he felt safe under Dugan's watchful gaze; he no longer felt alone.

"What I did was dumb," Bobby admitted to Dugan slowly. "I should've done what you told me and stayed below. I'm sorry. . . . Real sorry," he confessed. Dugan rumpled the boy's hair affectionately.

"We all do dumb things from time to time," Dugan said. "And I'm sorry, too. I came down pretty hard on you and Julie about the animals and about that dolphin out there, but that fish saved our lives."

"I named him Dodger, and he's not a fish," Julie reminded Dugan.

The man looked up and smiled. "You're right, he's a mammal, just like you and me. . . . Well," he

114

said, turning back to the boy, "I just want to say that I made a mistake and that I'm sorry. I'm just happy everyone's all right."

"I won't ever do anything like that again," Bobby promised.

"Good," Dugan smiled. They shook hands as if they were cementing a business deal. "Now, I want you to get some sleep," Dugan coaxed, pulling the covers up to the boy's chin. "We need you rested and ready; you're an important member of this crew!" Bobby smiled weakly, already close to dozing. He drifted back into a peaceful sleep and lay calm and quiet for most of the afternoon.

Much relieved, Julie tiptoed over to a large barrel of water. Carefully, she ladled out enough water to fill a shallow pan and carried it out on deck, being very careful not to slosh any onto the floor.

Miss Lafleur stayed below with Dugan and Bobby, reading her Bible, giving thanks for their safety.

Hiro and Cleveland tended a small fire in the hibachi. Julie placed the pan over the fire and waited for it to heat up.

"How Bobby?" Cleveland asked.

"He's tired, but he's okay," she said with a smile of relief. The men smiled and bowed in response to the good news. Julie pushed her long hair back out of her way; a breeze had blown it across her face.

A breeze! they all realized at once. Instantly, the three scrambled to their stations. Cleveland and Julie adjusted the sail. Hiro manned the rudder and turned the ship expertly into the wind.

Dugan and Miss Lafleur came on deck, looking very happy. "Well, what do you know!" Dugan beamed. "This has turned into a pretty good day after all!"

Even Dodger, Julie's friendly porpoise, celebrated with them. He leaped out of the water, flipped over onto his back and slapped the waves with a loud and happy splash. As the boat moved ahead, the dolphin swam just ahead of the nose. It led the way, making graceful leaps and arcs into the water and spraying little geysers of water vapor into the air from the blowhole atop its head. Julie stood at the bow and cheered him on.

For the rest of the day and into the night, they sailed north-by-northwest, running before the wind, making the best time possible.

Julie sat at the stern beside Hiro and Cleveland. She stared ahead of the ship and watched a bright half-moon shine down on the water; the men worked the rudder and set their course by the stars. They sailed right at the moon on the horizon.

Suddenly, Julie realized the whole new world that the Japanese sailors headed toward! Men have walked on the moon and they don't even know it yet! she thought. Their country has changed. Their families have changed. Technologies and politics, customs and cultures. So many new things awaited them. And yet, the men sailed ahead. So determined, they appeared to Julie. So brave and ready to face whole new challenges and adventures. Each gives strength and confidence to the other. Each man relies upon the other, she realized, and that reliance is a good thing. A thing to be trusted. She felt anxious for the two old friends, but she knew they would succeed.

Later that night, Dugan, Miss Lafleur, Julie and

Bobby sat on the foredeck, sipping steaming cups of coffee. The glow of the hibachi embers warmed them slightly.

"The way I look at it," Dugan began, "we've got two days' worth of water, and even with the wind, we're getting nowhere fast." He looked around the circle. Bobby nodded seriously. He knew their situation was grave and that a new attempt at being rescued had to be made. But what to do? he wondered.

"To the best of our knowledge," Dugan continued, "we're still miles away from shipping lanes and airline flight routes. We might just as well be the only people on earth at this moment. . . ." Dugan's voice drifted off; he sounded tired and worried.

"Remember in the story of the *other* Noah's Ark?" Julie began slowly, an idea forming in her head.

"Go on," Miss Lafleur encouraged.

"Well, they were stuck out on the ocean for a long time, too, right?"

"Right," Bobby answered.

"And they didn't know where they were and they needed to find land, too, right?"

"Uh-huh."

"Well, the Noah in the Bible sent a dove off to fly ahead of them, remember?" asked the girl.

"Right!" Dugan shouted. Happily, he reached over and kissed Julie's forehead. "Julie, you might just have found the answer!"

"We don't have a dove, but we do have a *duck!*" Bobby understood and shared Dugan's excitement.

"We'll send him off first thing in the morning!" Dugan announced. "Let's make sure we give him a few extra vitamins in his breakfast tomorrow," Dugan joked. "That duck's got a long haul ahead of him!"

Dugan held the mallard drake in both hands, lifted it up to eye level and looked the green-headed bird straight in the face.

"Okay, duck," he began. Bobby and Julie giggled at the sight of Dugan actually talking to an animal! Dugan continued very seriously, "Listen up, now, because we need your help."

Dugan pointed the bird toward the horizon. "Out there, somewhere, is Hawaii. . . . Get that? Hawaii! Hula girls in grass skirts, luaus, flowers, sunny beaches and lots and lots of beautifully tanned lady ducks!" Even Cleveland laughed at the line.

Miss Lafleur reread the message she intended to affix to the bird's leg: "We are the survivors of Flight A-1-9 . . ." it began. Hiro and Cleveland had carefully worked out their coordinates from the positions of the stars and, in the note, the woman had given their location in degrees and minutes of latitude and longitude.

". . . Please help us," the message ended simply.

Julie helped to hold the bird still as Miss Lafleur rolled the strip of paper into a tube, slipped it onto the duck's leg and attached it securely, but not too tightly.

The nervous duck, unused to such treatment, kicked its legs and tried to wriggle free of Dugan's grasp. It snapped at the man's nose with its hard, fine-toothed bill, but Dugan was careful not to hurt the bird.

"Ready," Miss Lafleur announced.

Solemnly, Dugan walked to the very front of the bow and stood just over the glass-domed nose. The others followed him in silent procession. Ceremoniously, Dugan raised the bird high over his head and, with great cheers from everyone, he released the bird into the early-morning sky.

Julie and Bobby called and waved happily as the duck flew high over the deck. It stroked the wind with its wings and banked right. It flew in a big circle around them. Once, twice, it circled, as if it were trying to get its bearings, to establish a sense of direction. And then, just as it appeared that the duck was ready to venture out to sea, it fluttered to a roost on the crow's nest atop the mast!

"No!" Bobby called. In frustration, Dugan picked up an old engine bolt they had used as a sinker and took careful aim. But Bobby moved quickly as Julie and the others jumped and flapped their arms, trying to scare the bird away. The duck looked down at them and quacked defiantly.

Reaching the base of the mast, the boy began to climb upward, talking softly to the bird as he pulled himself higher and higher above the deck. Finally, he reached the crow's nest and sat at the edge, dangling his feet in the air. The duck waddled a little closer to the boy.

"Listen," Bobby began, "you and the other animals needed us and trusted us to take care of you, right?"

The duck nibbled at Bobby's pants leg.

"Well, I think we did a pretty good job." The

commotion on the deck stopped; everyone grew quiet and watched.

"Maybe not a *great* job, but we tried because you needed us." Bobby paused and looked down at the people below. "Now we need your help," he said softly. "Otherwise nobody's ever gonna make it home. . . ." And Bobby truly wanted them to be home. Somewhere!

Almost as if the bird understood Bobby's words, it hopped to the edge of the crow's nest, paused to test the breeze, and launched itself into the air! To the cheers of Bobby and Julie, the duck swooped low, out over the ocean. With a powerful beating of its wings, it streaked toward the horizon and skimmed just over the waves. It flew straight, unwaveringly, into the wind.

With a whoop of delight, Bobby scrambled down from the crow's nest and swung down to the deck by a rope. He joined the others' cheering. Only Dugan remained quiet. He followed the duck until it was only a speck in the sky.

"I just hope that note was written in Chinese, . . ." he deadpanned.

"Why?" asked Miss Lafleur, sensing the man's concern, stopping her happy waving.

" 'Cause Hawaii is *that* direction." He pointed at the horizon, away from where the duck had just flown off.

"Uh-oh. . . ." Cleveland said.

CHAPTER NINE

ALL day and all night they took turns searching the ocean with binoculars. One would stand at the bow as the other stood at the stern. Together, two people could cover the entire horizon, all the way around them.

Not once did anyone see any sign of rescue.

But by mid-morning the next day, Hiro spotted the darkness just over the surface in the distance. Black, shadowy. He signaled to Cleveland who turned his binoculars in that direction.

The men focused on a large mass of clouds moving toward them. Like huge, ominous mountains, they skimmed toward the boat. "I thought we spot land," Cleveland explained slowly, never taking his eyes away from the clouds in the distance. More and more piled behind the ones before them.

". . . But we got *storm* coming our way. Fast! And it a big one!" Instantly, everyone jumped into action. Bobby saw the thunderheads for the first time; they grew darker and bigger by the second!

Dugan and Miss Lafleur, not having enough time to roll up the sail, tore it down and stuffed it into the hold as quickly as they could. Hiro and Cleveland worked to lash to the deck anything they could not carry inside. Bobby and Julie ran supplies and tools from the deck into the hold. Thunder rumbled through the air.

The sky and the water turned steel gray. Waves slapped against the hull.

Dugan and Miss Lafleur stood over the opened bomb-bay doors, helping the others to climb inside. Once everyone was in the hold, Dugan and the woman took one last look around to make sure everything that could be done to protect them *had* been done.

"Can we do anything else?" she asked, staring at the rapidly approaching storm.

"Yeah, Bernie," Dugan said honestly. "Pray like crazy that if the waves don't kill us the sparks won't either!"

"Sparks?" she asked.

"That's an electrical storm, honey, and we're like one big lightning rod!" Dugan pushed her head back down the ladder and he followed her inside.

They pulled the doors shut and sealed them. The children tied the animals in their stalls and stowed loose objects securely. The ship began to rock in the waves. Bobby fought hard to contain his fear.

"Come on, Brutus!" Bobby strained, pulling on his halter. The bull was frightened by the sudden commotion, and he balked. "Come on, *please!*" He pulled hard with both hands. Finally, the bull let himself be tied in his stall.

A huge wave rolled the boat severely, throwing Dugan off balance. "Hang on!" he shouted. "This one's gonna be a doozie!" Another wave crashed into the hull. Melinda bellowed in fright. The wind whistled through the ropes overhead. The hull lurched up and down in the sea.

It hit at once. Wind. Rain. Lightning! Thunder. As if a gigantic hand had lifted the ship and shook it; animals, boxes, people, rattled around inside. The compartment was filled with screams of all kinds; the wind shrieked and the boat moaned and groaned against the attack.

They heard the sound of splintering wood; the mast had been snapped in half by the gale. It crashed down onto the deck and smashed the glass nose. Instantly, water gushed into the cockpit. Dugan, Cleveland and Hiro struggled to close the bulkhead hatch against the flood. Finally, it jammed shut and sealed. They stood ankle-deep in water and the nose began to tip down slightly as the cockpit filled with water.

The animals were in a panic. In addition to having to protect themselves, everyone tended to the livestock as well. Bobby tried to contain Brutus; the bull tugged at his ropes and slipped on the wet floor, frightening himself even more. "Okay, Brutus," Bobby tried, "easy now." But his words did little to calm the animal. He bellowed loudly.

A coconut-oil lantern rocked over atop a wooden crate. The burning oil spread over the top of the box. Miss Lafleur put out the flames by beating them with a blanket. Now smoke filled the air.

The animals struggled harder.

"Bobby!" shouted Miss Lafleur. The boy looked up to see a huge wooden crate, yanked from the wall, slide quickly toward him. The boy froze in fear. With a yell, Hiro tackled the boy and yanked him clear just as the crate rushed past, narrowly missing them and smashing into the metal bulkhead. Instantly, Dugan and Cleveland were upon it, lashing it to the wall.

The hull heaved in the storm. Julie slipped beneath Melinda's unsteady feet. Bobby dragged her clear.

For twenty long minutes, the storm raged around them and for twenty minutes the brave crew battled back. The masts, the deck and the rudder were torn from the fuselage by the waves.

And then it stopped. The storm was over.

Julie peered through the tail gunner's windows. "It's gone!" she announced. "It's over!" Bobby shouted over the sounds of the frightened animals. Dugan climbed up the ladder and forced open one of the bomb-bay doors. It was windy, but quiet. Dugan climbed up and out of the hold. Below him, he could hear Brutus' angry bellowings, but paid no attention to them. The storm was over! They had survived. He stood quietly and watched the thunderheads roll off into the distance and heard the rumblings of far-off thunder. The sky grew lighter.

Crash! Dugan heard the sounds from below.

"Brutus!" Bobby shouted, frightened and concerned. Dugan raced back down the ladder and dropped into the hold.

Brutus had ripped himself free from his tether rope and trampled his stall. He bellowed and kicked and stomped a front hoof. Julie, Miss Lafleur, Cleveland and Hiro crowded into the far corner. Bobby trembled and moved slowly toward the raging bull. "Easy, Brutus," he tried, "calm down now. . . ." Brutus refused to face the boy; he shook his massive head, lowered his horns and rammed into a wooden crate. The box burst open, scattering tools around the floor. The ax slid toward Dugan; Hiro's old pistol clattered into a corner. Suddenly, Brutus turned toward Bobby and snorted once. Bobby saw rage in the bull's eye. Slowly, the horns lowered.

"Stop!" Dugan hollered from behind the bull. Brutus faced the man and charged! Dugan dove toward the ax, but the bull's massive head slammed into Dugan's side and threw him against the bulkhead. One horn caught him under his arm. Dugan lay on the floor, bleeding, unconscious. Brutus pawed the floor, ready to strike again. Bobby scrambled to the corner, pushing animals out of the way, searching the floor with his hands. Brutus tensed, ready to lunge forward and finish off Dugan once and for all.

"No!" Bobby shrieked at the bull. Brutus caught the boy out of the corner of one eye. Bobby knelt on the floor, trembling. He faced the bull head-on

125

with both hands held at arm's length in front of him. He aimed Hiro's pistol straight at the bull. His voice came in painful sobs.

"Stop it, Brutus!" he pleaded, with tears flooding his eyes. The barrel of the gun remained steady although the rest of the boy shivered with fear and anguish. "He didn't mean it," Bobby tried to explain. "He tried to protect us. He was scared—like you were scared," Bobby sobbed. Brutus perked his ears and cocked his head.

Bobby cocked his gun.

"We have to stop this," Bobby pleaded. There was silence and stillness around him. He heard the bull breathing heavily, panting.

Tears streamed down the boy's cheeks. "We have to protect each other."

Behind the boy, Melinda mooed once softly. Brutus swung his heavy head toward her and took a slow step toward her side. He looked exhausted.

"Oh, thank God!" Miss Lafleur exhaled. She had held her breath throughout the ordeal. She and Julie rushed to Dugan's side and began to revive him.

Bobby sat on the floor, let the gun drop to his side and leaned his head against the wall. He stared blankly at the floor and sighed deeply.

Brutus nuzzled his mate as if nothing had ever happened, and Bobby felt the warm sun streaming in from the opened doors. The sky had cleared.

Dugan groaned and shook his head, trying to focus his eyes. He looked to the woman, then to Julie. "Where's Bobby?" he asked quickly. He sat up and winced in pain, but he smiled when he saw that the boy was all right.

Dugan inched his way to Bobby's side. "You okay?" he asked softly.

Bobby nodded. "You?" the boy asked.

Dugan touched his ribs and checked his fingertips; he was not bleeding badly. "I'll live," he said, smiling.

Bobby smiled back. "Good!"

The voice seemed to come from out of nowhere. "Attention! Crew of Flight A-One-Niner! Prepare to come alongside!"

"What the—?!" Dugan shouted. He helped Bobby to his feet, and the two hurried up the ladder to the listing deck.

"Come on, Bernie!" Dugan called. Miss Lafleur and the rest hurried right behind.

Standing out on the battered deck, they looked up at the broadside of a three-hundred-foot Coast Guard cutter! The uniformed crewmen lined the railings of the decks and stared down at the crumpled, partially submerged vessel.

"Noah's Ark?" an officer called down through the amplified hailer. It seemed that everyone on the ship stared at them in total disbelief.

Exhausted, tattered, soaked, sunburned, hungry, bruised and emotionally drained, Bobby, Julie and the others gazed silently up at the towering ship.

As if in shock, Dugan pulled off his cap and let it hang in his hand. He stared up at the captain of the cutter. "Permission to come aboard?" Dugan gasped.

"Permission granted!" came the reply from the uniformed officer.

Perched on the railing beside the captain, they saw a very proud-looking duck. He shook his head in a flutter of green feathers and quacked once as if to say, "I told you so!"

The crisply clean, cool sheets felt wonderful to Bobby. Even the narrow, squeaky, lumpy mattress on the bunk felt good to the boy as he stretched out in his very own cabin. He stared out the porthole beside his bed and gazed out at the night.

The animals had been transferred to a subdeck on the cutter. Every one had been carefully fed and watered and cared for. Only then had Bobby agreed to let himself be attended to. He and the others were bathed and clothed and fed by the very gracious Coast Guardsmen. Bobby lay on his back, his hands behind his head, smiling to himself. He remembered the captain's amazement at Dugan's introducing him to Hiro and Cleveland. "Wait 'til they hear this at home!" the officer had said to himself as he bowed to them.

"And how!" Cleveland had returned. Bobby chuckled at the remembrance. A light knock came at his door.

"Come in," the boy said softly. Dugan stood in the doorway.

"Okay if we talk?" the man asked. "You're not asleep yet, are you?"

"Nope," Bobby answered, moving over a bit on the bed for Dugan to sit down.

Not knowing quite what to do, Dugan smiled self-consciously and motioned to the ship. "Sure a lot fancier than the 'Ark,' eh?" he kidded. Dugan stepped into the room and sat on the corner of the bed.

"Tonight," Dugan began slowly, "after they radioed to the world that we all were okay . . ."

"Yeah?" Bobby listened closely.

". . . Well, I got to thinking maybe we really *were* going to make it to Hawaii after all." Bobby nodded. ". . . Then I got to thinking, 'Where're we going *after* we get to Hawaii?' " Dugan continued.

"Home, I guess," Bobby said almost sadly.

Dugan held up a finger. "Ah, but where's *that?*" he asked like a comic professor. Bobby shrugged.

"Listen, here's what I think. I think we started out to get someplace and to do something, you follow me? The animals? The islanders? The airplane? All that?"

Bobby nodded. "Yeah, I understand."

"Well, I think, after all we've been through, the least we could do is finish what we were supposed to do in the first place."

"Go to Makuarana and deliver the animals?" Bobby asked, feeling suddenly a little excited.

"Yeah! What do you think?"

"Sure!" Bobby smiled.

"I think Bernie should have the chance to help those people like she wants to. And I want to help her."

"Get to Makuarana?" Bobby asked, his hopes rising.

129

"Yeah. . . . I figure the two of us make a pretty good team," Dugan answered.

"*Two?*" Bobby asked. He felt hurt, almost abandoned.

"What I meant was—"

"What about Julie and me?!" Bobby snapped.

"Wait a minute—"

"Where's *our* home?"

"Kid, that's not what I—"

"You want to marry her, don't you?" Bobby cut in. Dugan nodded. "And she wants to, too?" Bobby asked, feeling a twinge of pain when Dugan nodded again.

Julie surprised Bobby by stepping into the room. "And what are *you* gonna do for Miss Lafleur?" she asked Dugan, frankly. She had heard the whole conversation.

"Well," Dugan began to explain, "in Hawaii, I figure I can scrape together enough money to get us a ride on a freighter from Honolulu. . . . We can get there and get settled on Makuarana in no time at all!" Bobby watched how seriously Julie talked to Dugan. It was almost as if she were bargaining with the man, he thought.

Miss Lafleur's voice came in from the hallway. "But you would not have to return to the orphanage for long," the woman said to the girl. "Only until we get settled."

"Not good enough." Julie shook her head. Suddenly, Bobby realized that Julie was setting the terms to a four-way agreement! They never even had *considered* abandoning him!

"Julie's right," Bobby joined in, "we got into this thing together from the beginning and we're sticking together all the way through to the end." He and Julie nodded to each other with determination.

"If you want our blessings on your getting married tomorrow morning. . . ." Julie's and Bobby's terms were final.

Dugan and Miss Lafleur looked at each other, smiled, and looked back at Julie and Bobby.

"Okay," Dugan said with a grin. "Deal!"

Bobby and Julie shook hands before rushing to embrace Dugan and Bernie. Bobby had never felt happier. Julie had never been so certain.

"Dugan?" Bobby whispered.

"What?" the man came near and whispered back.

Bobby dug through the pockets of his clothes and found his special suede pouch: the one in which he kept his mother's ring. Bobby handed it to Dugan.

"You're gonna need this tomorrow morning," said the boy with a smile. Dugan accepted it sincerely.

"Thanks, kid."

"You're welcome," said the boy.

The next morning, as the shining Coast Guard cutter cruised into Honolulu harbor, it attracted quite a bit of attention. Boats of all shapes and sizes cruised close to see the strange "Ark" the cutter towed behind it.

A herd of barnyard animals stood out on the rear deck of the Coast Guard vessel; they basked in the morning sun.

And on the foredeck of the ship, everyone in the

harbor could watch a military wedding! Lines of uniformed Guardsmen attending the ceremony gleamed in the sun.

"Do you, Noah, take Bernadette . . ." the chaplain began.

Bobby stood beside Dugan throughout the ceremony.

Julie so honored Bernadette.

Hiro and Cleveland acted as proud fathers and bowed to each other, happily.

Brutus and Melinda stood behind the old sailors and surveyed the scene contentedly.

". . . By the power invested in me as chaplain in the United States Navy, I now pronounce you man and wife . . ." the berobed man concluded with a smile. "You may kiss the bride, Captain Dugan." And Dugan turned to Bernadette. He leaned forward and he kissed her gently.

As if every vehicle afloat were waiting for the cue, the people of the beautiful harbor signaled their congratulations and best wishes by cheering, applauding, revving the engines of their boats, sounding their horns and whistles and sirens. From a huge luxury yacht, fireworks arched from the main deck and burst over the steep green hills that surrounded them. The happy people aboard a gigantic ocean liner cast fragrant orchids and beautiful leis onto the deck of the cutter. The flower necklaces landed over everyone, even Brutus and Melinda! Dugan and Bernie held each other for the longest while.

Reaching out to the children, they embraced them as their own.

"And they lived happily ever after?" Bobby called out to Julie over the sounds of celebration.

Julie smiled, stuck her hands into her back pockets, and shrugged her shoulders.

"I'd bet on it!" she called out happily.

Bobby reached for Julie's hand.

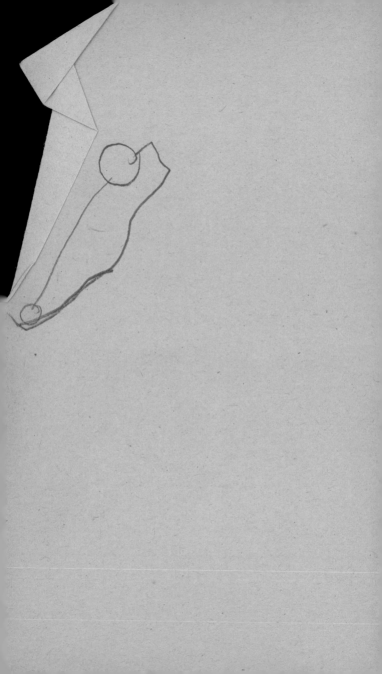